WAITING FOR THE SUN

PATRICK IOVINELLI

World Castle Publishing, LLC
Pensacola, Florida
Copyright © Patrick Iovinelli 2016
Paperback ISBN: 9781629895727
eBook ISBN: 9781629895734
First Edition World Castle Publishing, LLC. November 14, 2016
http://www.worldcastlepublishing.com

Cover: Karen Fuller
Editor: Lisa Petrocelli

CHAPTER ONE

Wilton is a shit town. Ma and I live in a creaky, yellow frame house just two blocks from Chesapeake Bay. My brother Brian and I counted the steps once. It was 1,107 steps from our front door to the water during low tide. Of course, it'd be less during high tide.

Ma's had the house since before Brian and I were born. She and our dad bought it when they were first married and he was the head of maintenance at Wilton Heights, one of the two big resorts in town. The other big resort is called the Champagne. They're sort of run-down now, but these two resorts pretty much provide jobs to all the people who live around here. They were both a big deal when they were built in the 50s, and even though people don't come like they used to, they're still a big part of the town. Even the people who

3

don't work at the resorts usually work at the bars and restaurants around them.

Our house was in horrible shape when my parents bought it, but it was cheap and it was close to Dad's job at the resort. Dad figured he could fix it up over the next few years and really get his money's worth. Unfortunately, it didn't turn out that way.

Our dad ran off when I was only two. It turns out he was banging one of the waitresses who worked in the bar at Wilton Heights. Ma doesn't talk about it much, but a couple of years ago, she told me she heard that our dad and the waitress moved to Tampa. She said she wasn't sure if it was true, though. He's never come back around or sent us anything. I don't really even remember him. Brian does. Sometimes, when he's drunk or high, Brian talks about Dad. He talks about stuff he did with him—like playing catch or going fishing off the pier. I was too little to have ever done any of that stuff with him.

I don't really care.

Since Dad ran off, Ma has had a few boyfriends. Most of them were waiters or cooks in Kracker's, the restaurant she used to work at. A few of them worked in the resorts, too. She even married one of the resort guys, Dan Howe, who was a groundskeeper at the Champagne. Ma was crazy about Dan. He was a little younger than Ma—tall and with a thick, brown beard. He wasn't a bad guy either, but he liked to drink and go on motorcycle trips with his buddies, and he hated Brian. That's what drove Dan and Ma apart. I think Dan just couldn't take Brian's shit anymore.

My brother has had problems his whole life. Brian gets real mad sometimes, and he just can't control himself. He's gotten in tons of fights. He's been suspended from school about ten times over the years. The social workers were always calling our house, wanting to put Brian in group therapy sessions or something, but Ma never let them. She always protected him. No matter what Brian did, Ma would go to school and argue with the counselors and principals until they'd finally let Brian come back. Brian finally dropped out last year, which would've been his senior year. It's actually a miracle he made it as long as he did. School just wasn't his thing.

It's been harder the last few years because as Brian got older, the cops got involved. Brian never did anything really horrible, but he'd broken into stores and trashed them. He'd gotten into fights with cops about playing the music too loud in his truck—stuff like that. He just couldn't stay out of trouble.

Ma always bailed him out, though. Even the few times that things were more serious, she saw it as her duty to protect him from all the people who were treating him like he was crazy. Bipolar was the word they always used, but Ma said that was just another word for crazy and if we let the school or the juvenile corrections counselor label him that way, he would be branded for the rest of his life.

I remember one time, Dan and Ma screaming at each other after the cops called and told Dan that Brian had been arrested again. Ma told Dan that if he didn't like her son, he could get the hell out. So he did. I don't think Ma ever forgave Brian for that.

I never told Brian this, but I actually kind of liked Dan. He never went out of his way to do anything with me or try to be my father, but if I was sitting on the couch with a book, he would ask me what I was reading. At first, I would just tell him the title of the book and then give him a short summary of the plot. But each time he asked, I went a little farther. I'd tell him a little more about the book and even sneak in some of my opinions. And he was cool about it. Even if he was about to leave or something, he would always stand there and listen until I was done talking. There were a couple of times he even asked me questions about something in the book. It wasn't really a big deal, but Brian and Ma never asked.

Dan Howe—that's who I was thinking about at dinner on my fifteenth birthday.

Ma and I were sitting at the scrubbed kitchen table. I was sawing into my second chicken breast while Ma sat, her plate untouched, slouched in the chair across from me. A Winston dangled from her lip.

"What are ya thinking about, Nate?" she asked.

"Nothing," I said.

"You haven't said nothing this whole time."

I put my knife and fork down. "What do you want to talk about, Ma?"

"I dunno. Something. Anything," she said.

"How are you feeling today?" I asked.

"I don't want to talk about that."

"It's been three days since the last treatment. You should be eating at least a little by now."

"I can't. I try. I take a few bites, but then I feel like I wanna throw up," she said.

"This second round of chemo has really kicked your ass, huh?"

"It's your birthday, honey. Let's not talk about this. How's school? Are you reading anything good?"

Boy, Ma must've been desperate. "Yeah, I

guess," I said. "I've been reading those stories of the ancient Greeks. I just read the labors of Hercules. Did you know that he did all those heroic things, killing monsters and stuff, because he was trying to make up for killing his family? He went crazy one day and killed his wife and kids. He had to do the labors to make up for that."

I looked up at Ma. She wasn't listening. She was looking down at her nails.

I went back to my chicken. We sat there in silence for a few minutes.

I had been waiting for it, but it still hit me when she finally asked, "So have you seen your brother lately?"

"Two days ago." I didn't look up from my food.

"How is he?" I felt Ma's eyes searching my face as she asked.

"He's fine, Ma."

"Where's he staying?" she asked.

"He's staying with one of his friends," I said quickly.

Ma laughed. "No, he's not. Whaddaya think I'm stupid or something?"

I kept chewing my chicken. I kept my eyes down when I reached out for my water.

"I know he stays by her house," she said.

I finally looked up. "Yeah, Ma. Sometimes he

does."

We stared at each other for a few moments. I could tell that Ma wanted to go on her whole rant about how Brian shouldn't be sleeping at his girlfriend Shannon's house and how one day her father was going to catch Brian and string him up by the balls. I'd heard it a thousand times before. I just wasn't in the mood for it tonight.

Ma seemed to sense my weariness with the subject. She stubbed out her cigarette.

"Did you invite him to dinner tonight like I told you?" she asked instead.

"Yeah. He said he might come," I said.

As if on cue, there was a knock on the door. Ma turned slowly and made like she was going to try and get up. She put her hands on her knees to push off. I sprang from my seat.

"I got it, Ma."

I opened the door and there was Brian. His long blond hair fell onto the shoulders of his green and black rugby polo. He had a box wrapped in newspaper under his arm. He was grinning at me like he did when we were kids. It was charming. His lip sort of curled and his eyes held a laugh like he was waiting to get to the punch line of a joke.

When I was little, I learned to become wary of that smile. It usually meant Brian had played a joke on me and he was just waiting for me to discover it. I remember one time when I was seven and he was about ten, we were about to go to bed. Brian kept milling about the room, pretending to pick up his schoolbooks and organize his folders. All the while he was sneaking peeks at me as I was about to get in bed.

I'd finally had enough and asked him, "What is with you?"

He could barely contain his excitement. "Nothing," he said, between giggling breaths he was trying to suppress.

I finally flopped onto my bed and as I plopped my head on the pillow, I heard a squishy explosion and felt something slimy and wet all over my head and neck. Brian had snuck the leftover lemon meringue pie out of the fridge, taken it out of the tin, and spread it smoothly on my pillow inside the pillowcase.

As I sat up, trying to figure out what the hell was all over me, Brian was hunched over, hands on his knees, laughing. He thought his prank was so funny that it didn't even make him mad when I picked up the pillow and whipped it at him. It hit him in the shoulder and a little bit of the whipped cream splattered on his shirt.

Needless to say, after that I was always leery

when Brian was grinning.

"What's up, Turd?" he said and hugged me around the neck.

I started laughing and hugged him back.

"Happy birthday, little bro." He held out the present.

"Thanks, Bri," I said and carried it back over to the table.

Brian didn't move. He looked down at Ma who was staring at him. The smile left his face.

"Hi, Ma."

"Do I look that bad?" she said.

Brian looked past her at me. I nodded toward Ma.

"No, Ma. You look good." Brian was always the worst liar. He hadn't been home since Ma started her second round of chemo. He took a couple of tentative steps toward the table.

"Come and eat with us. I made enough to feed a football team," Ma said.

Brian sat down on the chair between us. Ma got up and started slowly toward the stove.

"I'll get it, Ma." I got to my feet again.

"You sit down. It's your birthday," she said, waving me back in to my seat.

Once she'd fixed Brian a plate, she turned awkwardly to bring it back to the table. She fell to

11

one knee and the plate slipped from her grasp.

"Ma!" I ran over to her.

"The goddamned thing is so heavy." Ma had to pick up the plate with both hands.

"No, it's not, Ma. You just have to build up your strength," I said as I took the dish from her.

"I'll clean this up," she said.

"No, I got it. Why don't we sit you on the couch?" I said.

I lifted her and walked her over to the couch. She barely turned but I was able to push her into the seat. Then I got the paper towel and started to pick up the food Ma had spilled.

"Why don't you help him?" Ma said to Brian, who had been staring at her. "Nathan does everything around here. Not like you, who'd rather sleep in someone's basement than help out around his own mother's house."

"I don't mind helping out. I just don't wanna be around you," Brian said as he got up. By the time Brian reached me, I'd cleaned the spill. So he just stood over the spot, looking everywhere around the room except at Ma.

"Here, make yourself a plate." I jammed a fresh plate into Brian's hands. He stood there for a moment. When he looked at me, I could see that he was seething. I thought for a second he might take the plate and fling it at Ma.

"Go ahead," I said.

Brian stomped over to the stove and busied himself with the plate.

He stomped back over to the table, slammed the plate down, and began to shovel the food in his mouth.

"Haven't you ever eaten before?" Ma said.

"Ma, ease off," I said.

We sat in silence for a while. After a couple of minutes, Brian slowed down and started eating like a human. When I finally looked up, Ma had nodded off on the couch. I kicked Brian under the table. When he looked at me, I nodded over at Ma.

He looked over at her and his features relaxed.

"Jesus Christ, does she hate me," he whispered.

"She doesn't hate you. She's just mad is all."

"What the hell for?" he said.

"I don't know, Bri." I sighed. "Just cut her some slack, would ya? This round is really beating her up. She's not eating much and she's in pain a lot of the time."

"I can see that," he said. "Why?"

"The doctor said her body's run-down. Chemo kills cancer cells, but it also kills plenty of healthy cells, too. He told me that's why she gets weak and sick so much sooner after the treatments than the last round. Remember the first round? She would go a week or so after a treatment before the chemo made her sick. Then it would only last a day or two. This time, it hit her right after the first treatment and she hasn't really gotten better since then."

"Jesus! How come you didn't tell me?"

"What could you do, Bri? I knew it'd just make you feel bad," I said immediately. "This is just the way it's gotta be right now."

"She can't do much, huh?"

I shook my head. "Naw. Even tonight, she told me she was gonna make my birthday dinner. She couldn't even get the bag of chicken open. She stood there most of the time, but I had to do most of the work. She's real weak."

Brian looked over at her. I could tell he was in shock seeing her like this.

"So what'd you bring me?" I said between mouthfuls.

Brian finally took his eyes off Ma and reached across the table to put the box in front of me. I put my plate aside and tore off the newspaper.

"Sorry about the wrapping," Brian said. "Shannon's mother keeps the wrapping paper under her bed, so Shannon didn't want to try and sneak in there to get it this morning. We came real close to getting caught a couple of days ago, so we're trying not to push it."

"What happened?"

"I snuck into the basement around eleven, after her parents went to bed and we went at it for a while. Then, Shannon and I fell asleep on the couch. All of a sudden, the door opens from upstairs and someone starts coming down. Luckily, Shannon woke up as soon as the door clicked. She threw the blanket over me and ran over to the stairs. It was her dad. He asked what she was doing. He said he had gotten up to pee and saw that she wasn't in her room, so he came down to look for her. She told him she'd fallen asleep while she was watching a movie down there and had just woken up. All the time she's talking to her dad, I'm dead asleep ten feet away on the couch." Brian laughed. "If I'd started snoring, we'd have been caught for sure."

"Well, isn't that a lovely, romantic story?" Ma said. Her eyes were still closed. "You have no idea how proud a mother I am."

"C'mon, Ma," I said.

"Can't you ever just lay off?" Brian stood up angrily.

"You know you shouldn't be sneaking around and sleeping with that girl," she said.

"Her name is Shannon, Ma. And I love her. I've loved her since I was thirteen," Brian yelled.

15

Ma opened her eyes. For a moment, the hardness vanished from her face. "I know you love her. That's not the point. She's a good girl from a good family, Brian."

"So what, I'm not good enough for her?" I could tell that Brian was a few seconds from losing it completely.

"No, it's not that. She's gonna graduate from high school and go to college. She's gonna meet all sorts of boys who are smart and kind. Then there's you. You can't hold a job, you get in all sorts of trouble. Did you know that animal control lady still comes around every couple of weeks after what you did to that cat last year? What goes through your head sometimes?" Ma waved her lighter in Brian's direction.

"I only bashed it because it scratched my face — ☐ Brian tried to explain, but Ma wasn't listening. She just kept going.

"You can't even date her right — you have to go sneaking around. What kind of future do you think you and Shannon are gonna have if you don't get your shit together?" Ma said.

I looked up at Brian. His hands were balled into fists and he was breathing hard. I got up and walked in front of him, blocking Ma from his sight. "You better go, bro."

Brian's shoulder banged me hard as he stalked out the door.

"Someone has to tell him the way things are," Ma said.

I sighed and went over to clear the dishes.

CHAPTER TWO

Two nights later, I was mopping the floor in Maltby's Ice Cream Shop. It's my part-time job. It's pretty easy work—serving customers, stocking product, cleaning up. Maltby's is just a little storefront in the middle of Wilton's main street. It's a small shop and it never gets super-busy. That's why there's usually only one or two of us working at a time. It was Friday night and I was working with Dylan.

He's a cool kid. He's this gangly metalhead with long brown hair. His hair is even longer than Brian's. He's got to wear a hairnet at work. Every time the shop is empty, he blasts Metallica or Slayer or something. He doesn't do much work, really. I usually handle all the stocking and clean-up. He handles the customers pretty well, though. Selling is his thing. He makes his real money selling weed.

He's nothing big. Just enough to get by. That's how he knows Brian. He's been selling to my brother since they were in eighth grade.

It was nine o'clock and I'd just locked the door and started mopping the front. Dylan had taken off his hairnet and was banging his head behind the counter to "Cemetery Gates" by Pantera. I could see his brown hair flopping back and forth through the display glass above the buckets of ice cream.

Since Dylan had the music blasting, I couldn't hear the knocking on the door. When I finally turned around, I saw Maggie Cullen, Dylan's girlfriend, standing at the door. She had her arms out and this look on her face like, "What the fuck?"

I opened the door and she came in. There was a cinnamon scent in the air when she walked by.

"I've been banging on the door for like, five minutes," she said, looking from me over to Dylan. Dylan launched himself over the narrow counter space between the glass cases and picked Maggie up, crushing his lips against her neck.

He spun Maggie around and she laughed. Her short floral dress floated out from around her. I'd stopped mopping and was watching them. Maggie noticed, and when Dylan placed her on the ground, she playfully pushed him away.

"C'mon now, Dyl. We're gonna make Nate jealous," she said.

I started mopping again.

"Oh, don't worry. I'll share ya with Nate." He looked over at me. "You just gotta let me go first," Dylan said.

"You're so bad," Maggie said, laughing.

"You going to Shannon's party?" Dylan asked.

"Yeah. I gotta go home first and do some stuff, but I'll be around later," I said.

"Yeah, we're probably gonna stop off at the beach first before we head over there," Dylan said. He nodded his head at Maggie.

Maggie punched him in the shoulder. "Hey, do you have to tell everyone where we do it?"

"No worries, babe. Nate won't come barging in on us," he said.

Maggie put her arms around Dylan's neck. "It's too cold for the beach, anyway."

The first time I'd worked with Dylan, about six months ago, he'd come to work really high and really chatty. That day he told me all about selling weed, dropping out of community college, and how he and Maggie would always go to this cave just off the beach down at Wilton Harbor. It was sort of out of the way and since you had to get down on your hands and knees to crawl into it, most people didn't even know it was there. He told me that his older brother had shown it to him and that the first time he took Maggie there was their first time. According to Dylan, now they go there all the time, at least until the fall.

I'd tried to find the cave once when I went to the beach with Brian and Shannon, but I couldn't. When I told Dylan where I'd been looking, he'd said, "No. You were too close to the parking lot. It's sort of halfway between the beach and the lot."

Dylan tossed his apron on the counter and put his arm around Maggie.

"Later, Nater," he said as they walked out.

He was funny, but it was kind of a douche move to leave at 9:01 without doing anything. He didn't even empty his register. I took out the cash and receipts, put them in the envelope, filled out the front part with the date, the amount, and dropped it in the safe slot. Then I hung up both of our aprons and finished mopping. Then I shut off all the lights, made sure all the doors were locked, all the freezers were closed, and I went out the back into the alley.

It was a nice night, so I'd walked. When I got home, the house was in pretty good shape. Ma was snoring in her bed and there were only a couple of dishes in the sink. Once I took care of those, I took a shower and put on a clean shirt for the party.

Twenty minutes later, I was parallel parking Ma's van about two blocks down from Shannon's house. You could tell this was going to be a rager. I'd driven right up to the house and the porch was full of people. In fact, there wasn't enough room, so some of them spilled out onto the lawn. And there wasn't a single space to park on either side of her block or the next one. I guess I shouldn't have been surprised. Shannon was one of the most popular kids at Wilton High.

Shannon's house is in the center of town, away from the water. It's a yellow Colonial with a huge front porch. That's one of the reasons I think Wilton is such a dump. In most coastal towns, all the big, expensive houses are right on the water and the rest of the town is sort of normal. Not in Wilton. Here, all the fancy houses, like Shannon's, are the ones farthest away from the bay. It seems like the poorer you are, the closer you live to the water. I think the rich folks hope that one day the ocean will swallow us all up. I can't really blame them.

All the lights were on and I could hear chatter and music from half a block down as I walked toward Shannon's. My hands were in my pockets as I weaved through the people on the lawn and the porch. I recognized most of the faces from school, but I didn't say anything to anyone. Some dude with a Mohawk nodded at me as I reached the front door—I think he was in my algebra class last year. I nodded back.

When I got into the house, I could see that most of the first floor was empty. There were a few people sitting on chairs or couches, talking or making out, but I could see a big crowd in the backyard through the screen door and I could hear all sorts of talking, singing, and yelling from the basement. That's usually where all the shit went down.

When I got to the bottom of the stairs, it took a minute for my eyes to adjust to the darkness and the smoke, but I heard Brian's voice right away.

"What the fuck are you doing here?" At first I smiled, thinking that Brian was welcoming me with one of his signature phrases, but then I saw the ring of people standing around Brian and Joe Runnel.

"Just having a good time," Joe Runnel said. He was a burly senior with a crew cut. He was standing there with his thumbs hooked in his jeans pockets staring at Brian. There was a sort of sly grin on his fleshy face. He was half a foot taller than Brian was, and he had about fifty pounds on him.

Brian was standing a few feet in front of him, looking up into his face. I could see Brian's hands were already balled into fists. Brian hated Joe

Runnel. Brian had been dating Shannon since she was in the eighth grade, but they'd broken up a lot, too. And Shannon had dated Joe a couple of different times when she was broken up from Brian.

"Shannon invited me, bro," Joe said. "You know she can't get enough."

Joe Runnel had barely gotten the last word out when Brian's fist hit his face. Joe didn't even have to time to react because Brian immediately grabbed his head and brought it crashing into his knee.

A second later, Joe Runnel was on his back and his arms were splayed out to his sides. He was already out cold. Brian knelt on his chest and began pummeling his face. I ran the rest of the way down the steps and shoved Brian off of him.

Brian popped up immediately and grabbed for my head.

"You're gonna kill him," I shouted.

He pushed me back so he could extend his arm for a punch. Then suddenly his eyes lit with recognition.

"Nate, what the hell are you doing?" he said, still holding on to my collar.

"You're gonna kill him, fuckhead," I said. "He's already out. Everyone else would've stood here watching while you pounded his nose back into his brain." I shoved Brian's hand off my shirt.

"You think I could really do that?" he asked. Then he laughed. So did a bunch of the people around him. After a few seconds, even I cracked a smile. Brian reached out and pulled me into a bear hug. I stopped smiling when I looked over Brian's shoulder and saw Shannon coming down the stairs.

Shannon was wearing jean shorts and a tank top tied off to reveal the smooth, tan skin of her belly. Her wavy blonde hair fell on her shoulders and there was just a hint of glistening sweat on her forehead. She'd probably been dancing with her girlfriends in the backyard when she heard all the commotion.

"What's going on?" she said directly to me.

Brian turned around and held his arm over my shoulders. "Hey, babe, I was just welcoming baby bro to the party," Brian said with a broad grin.

Shannon knew Brian well enough to know that something was wrong. She came forward and pushed Brian and me apart. She then looked down at Joe Runnel, his face bloody, unconscious on the floor. She knelt down and reached out her hands to touch him, but kept them just an inch or two away from his body. It was like she wasn't sure if she'd hurt him more if she touched him.

"What did you do?" she screamed over her shoulder.

25

"Your boyfriend here was trying to have a good time, so I gave him one," Brian said as he walked over to the couch.

"Brian, he's completely unconscious," Shannon said, kneeling before him.

Someone handed Brian a joint. "Yeah, he's lucky he'll ever wake up again," Brian shot back.

Shannon craned her neck to look at Brian. "What is wrong with you?"

"Nothing's wrong with me. I'm not the one who invited my boyfriend to her house so he could get his ass kicked," Brian said, crossing his legs. Word had spread that there was trouble in the basement. Kids were lining the staircase up to the kitchen. Most of them were whispering, passing the news on to the main level of the house.

"He's not my boyfriend, psycho. I thought you were," she said. Shannon turned back to Joe Runnel.

Brian stood up and kicked the coffee table. It skidded across the basement floor. "Then what the hell is he doing here?"

"I don't know," Shannon said quietly. "I didn't invite him. Honest." She still hadn't turned around to look at Brian. In fact, I noticed that her eyes were closed. Nobody else probably did.

"Like hell," Brian said.

"Ease up, Bri," I said.

"Stay out of it, Nate." Brian sat down, but still glared at Shannon's back.

Just then, Joe Runnel started to move. He groaned and curled himself on his side. Someone knelt down and started talking to him. After a few moments, two boys helped him to his feet. Joe's eye was already swollen shut—probably from Brian's knee—and he walked as if every movement was nothing but pain.

As the boys ushered him toward the stairs, Joe deliberately avoided looking at my brother.

"Have a good night, lover boy," Brian yelled once Joe was up the stairs. Everyone in the basement laughed except for Shannon and me.

"Everyone get out of here," Shannon said, standing up.

There was some groaning and chatter at this. I even heard one kid say, "But this party was just getting good."

"Out!" Shannon screamed, pointing to the stairs. People slowly started to move toward them. Brian sat on the couch, his legs crossed and his arms resting casually on the cushions.

"I'll get them out," I said to Shannon and walked past her toward the stairs.

"C'mon, let's go," I said to the kids who were taking their time up the stairs. "Party's over."

It took me about fifteen minutes to walk through the house and to get people moving. Most people were cool about it. They just downed their drinks and left their cups on tables and counters. One girl in a plaid skirt who I didn't recognize asked if I needed help throwing out all the garbage. "No, thanks. I'll get it," I said and ushered her toward the door with everyone else. Once I got everyone out, I started clearing up the cups and dumping out the ashtrays in the garbage. As I was working, I was listening for sounds from the basement. I expected to hear yelling at any moment.

When I was finally done, I threw the garbage out in the garage and came back into the house. I went to the basement door and started down the stairs. I still couldn't hear anything. I was about halfway down when I heard the grunting and the rustle of the couch fabric. I stood and listened for a few seconds. Right as I turned to go up the stairs, I heard Shannon whisper breathlessly, "You know you're the only one for me."

I closed the basement door quietly behind me and went to the fridge. As I reached for the handle, I saw a Post-it sticking on the freezer side, written in tidy, looping handwriting. It must've been a note from Shannon's mother.

It read, "Just checked your grades...Bring up

the B in Biology!" I couldn't imagine ever seeing a note like that on our refrigerator, but Shannon's parents were serious about her grades.

The party had ended both abruptly and early, so the fridge was still completely stocked with Budweiser and High Life. I took a High Life and went out to the yard. It was a dark, cloudless night. As I fell back into a beach chair, I just stared into that blackness.

About twenty minutes later, I heard the back door creak and footsteps in the grass behind me.

It was Shannon. "Did you do all the clean-up?" she asked.

"Everything I could."

"That's so sweet, Nate," she said. "Thanks."

I took another swig of the beer.

"Do you want another one? I'll have one with you out here," she said.

"What about Brian?"

"He fell asleep on the couch," she said, walking back toward the house.

When she came back out, she had a six-pack. She flopped down onto the chair next to mine and nudged my elbow with an icy bottle.

"What's the matter, Nate?"

I kept staring at the darkness.

"Is it your mother?" Shannon leaned forward

to look into my face.

I moved impatiently and took a swig of beer.

"I'm sorry, Nate. Brian was so upset when he came here a couple of nights ago. He said she looked like she was already dead and that he felt bad you were working so hard to take care of her. He kept saying he was a terrible son and that he wished he could fix things between him and your mom."

I swallowed hard. I didn't want to say anything. I didn't want to talk about this, but it just came rushing out all at once. "I wish they'd fix their shit, too. It's hard being Brian's goddamned brother, with him getting all angry and crazy all the time. And Ma isn't easy to be around either. She tries to be strong, but she's weak and I think she's really angry that this cancer and the chemo are kicking her ass. All she does is bitch at me about Brian, or about how she can't eat or drink, and that all she wants to do is smoke her Winstons. I'm just tired of it."

I could feel the pressure building in my chest and before I knew it, I was hunched over in the lawn chair, crying. Shannon came over and sat next to me on the chair. She put her arm around my shoulders. I could feel the soft brush of her hair against my cheek and smell her shampoo. It was some floral scent that reminded me of being outside after the rain.

"It's okay, Nate," she whispered. I could feel her breath in my ear.

"Ma's gonna die, Shan. And Brian is gonna go crazy and kill somebody," I said between sobs.

"No, Nate, it's gonna —" she started to say.

"Did you see him tonight?" I pulled away from her. "He'd have killed Joe Runnel if I hadn't stopped him. There's no off switch with him. He just keeps going until he's finally done being mad and he doesn't care what happens. How can you be with him?"

"What?" she said.

"How can you stand him?" I repeated. I think I must've been shouting by then.

"Calm down, Nate," she said as she patted my arm nervously.

We sat in silence for a few moments, but then Shannon said softly, "You know, your brother's not a bad guy."

I still wouldn't look at her. "Yeah, I know," I muttered.

"No, really. He's actually really sweet. Like the other day, when he came back from your house so upset, we stayed up that night talking. By the end of it, he told me that…" Her voice trailed off.

I finally looked up at her. There was a smile on her face as she thought about it. "He told you what?" I asked.

"He told me that I save his life every day."

I looked back down. I wasn't sure I wanted to hear any more.

"And he believes in me," she said.

"No, he doesn't. He almost killed Joe Runnel because he didn't believe you didn't invite him."

"No, Nate. He believes *in* me," Shannon said. "My parents are psycho about my grades because they want me to go to college, but they're on me all the time. My mother is always checking my grades and telling me I'm lazy, taking away my phone. But Brian...Brian always believes that I'll do fine. And I feel better then. It's like he thinks more of me than my own parents do."

"That's not true," I said. "I'm sure your mom and dad—"

She kept going as if she hadn't heard me interrupt her. "And I know he gets a little jealous or crazy sometimes, but he usually doesn't take it that far," she said, waving her hand toward the house.

"Yeah. I guess he usually doesn't," I said.

"And even if he does get really mad, I can usually get him to calm down after a while," she said.

"It's easy for you. All you gotta do is fuck him," I blurted out.

Shannon's eyes were wide as I looked at her. We sat in silence for what seemed like an eternity. I don't know which one of us was more shocked by what I'd just said.

All of a sudden, her lip twitched a little, and I could tell she was trying to suppress a smile. She couldn't. After a few seconds, she started to laugh. Her laugh was one of those short wheezing laughs that could take over a person's whole body in just a few seconds. Then I started to laugh. Pretty soon, we were both laughing so hard that neither of us could breathe. She leaned against me so she wouldn't fall over and I felt her cold hand rest on my collarbone. Then suddenly, her face was right in front of mine.

Without thinking, I kissed her quickly on the lips. We both stopped laughing. She was looking at me with even greater surprise than she had a minute earlier. I suddenly couldn't look up at her. I tried to find something interesting to stare at in the grass.

We sat in there for what seemed like an hour. I finally started to feel like I had to say something just to break that horrible silence.

"Shan, I'm sorry. I didn't mean to—" I stuttered.

"No, it's okay," she said.

"No, it's not. I never should have—"

She put her hand softly under my chin and lifted until my eyes met hers. They were brown with just a glint of gold in them.

"It's okay," she said.

I believed her.

"You won't tell Brian?"

"No, I most definitely won't tell Brian," she said.

"Thanks. You know, I better go." I stood up and patted my jeans to make sure I had my phone and my keys.

"Okay. Thanks for your help tonight," Shannon said.

I looked up at her quickly. "Yeah. You too," I said. Why the hell did I say that?

I turned quickly and headed for the gate.

"G'night, Nate," she called after me.

I stopped and turned to look back at her. She was sitting with her arms folded on the beach chair. She lifted one hand and gave me a shy, little wave. I waved back.

"G'bye, Shan."

CHAPTER THREE

When I opened my eyes, there was bright artificial light pouring in from the window of my room and I felt the early morning wind howling in my ears. Why the hell was the window open? I didn't remember opening it before I went to bed.

Then I felt something light hit me on the back of my neck and as it bounced in front of me, I saw a small brown puff fall to the floor. A second later, I felt another one. I flipped over and saw Brian, sitting in his old bed with a box of cereal. He was taking the puffs out one at a time and tossing them at me.

"What are you doing?" I covered my eyes to block out the light from the street.

"I'm trying to get one in your ear. Roll back on your side," he said. He was still in the same clothes he wore to the party the night before. Now that I thought about it, so was I.

"Cut it out, Bri."

Brian popped a puff in his mouth. "There's 'No-Fun Nathan' for you."

Brian pointed toward my bookshelf, where the box he'd given me on my birthday sat. I hadn't even torn all of the newspaper off of it yet. I'd only opened it far enough so I could get the present out of the box. "How do you like your present, No-Fun?" he asked.

"It's cool."

"Remember when we found it?" Brian got up and walked over to the shelf. He took the box, opened the flap, and slid the blade out of the box.

"Yeah, I remember," I said.

When Brian and I were little, we were always at the beach. We would go there early in the morning of every summer day, before anyone else in town was even awake, and play. Sometimes we'd play soccer in the sand. Other times, we played tag, using the water fountain as glue. Brian always caught me. Sometimes we'd make castles or forts in the sand. At first, we just made small ones for our toys. We'd carry our G.I. Joes in paper bags to the beach, but once Brian lost Roadblock, the heavy machine gunner, and probably his favorite figure, we stopped bringing toys to the beach.

After that, we tried to create forts for ourselves to play army in. It was usually a disaster. Either the tide would be too high, or we couldn't get the sand to pile up high enough, or else the beach got crowded and the lifeguard would tell us we had to let people put their towels and chairs in the spaces we were trying to build on. Even when we were little, it would piss Brian off something fierce. He hated when we'd have to give up. A lot of the time he'd argue with the lifeguards to let us keep working. As we got older, Brian's language got dirtier and there were several occasions when the lifeguards threatened to ban us from the beach entirely.

It never happened, though.

There was this one morning when we were going to build a huge fort that was going to be five feet high off the ground. Brian figured if it were big enough, the lifeguards wouldn't want to deal with having to knock it down and smooth out all the sand to let people occupy the space, and we'd get to leave it up and play in it until the tide rose and knocked it down.

Brian set our alarm clock for 4:30 a.m. We figured if we were going to build a fort that big, we'd need an early start. We reached the beach before five o'clock and started working. As the sun was coming up, I was digging up sand and bringing it over to Brian in two red plastic pails we had. At first, I used our plastic shovel, but that didn't work very well. So I started to scoop the sand in my hands and pour it in the pails. After one scoop, I felt a stinging in my hand and when I looked down, I saw blood streaked across my fingers.

I screamed and Brian ran over to me. He took me over to the water and washed my hand in the saltwater. It stung, but it cleared the blood and sand away. Once I saw how small the cut was, I stopped crying and felt better.

Brian was curious about what I cut my hand on, so we went over to the spot I'd been digging in and he started to slowly and carefully feel around in the sand.

"I think I feel something metal," he said.

A few seconds later, he pulled a long, rusted blade out of the sand.

"It's a knife," I said. "Who would leave a knife on the beach?"

Brian inspected it for a few moments. "It's not a knife. It's a bayonet."

"It's a what?" I said.

"A bayonet. Soldiers used to have these blades on the ends of their rifles, back like in the Civil War. When the enemy got close enough, he could stab him with it. This must be really old."

"Is it worth anything?" I asked. Even as kids, we knew we didn't have any money. Brian considered it for a moment, but once he ran his hand along the rusted blade, he shook his head.

"I doubt it," he said. "It's not in good shape."

"Well, I want it anyway," I said.

"Naw. You're too little. And besides, you already cut your hand on it."

"That's why it should be mine," I whined.

"I'll tell you what, you're right. It should be yours. But I don't trust you with it now. I'll hold on to it for you and when you're ready, I'll give it to you," he said.

I screamed and cried and threatened to tell our mother on him, but Brian wouldn't budge. He wouldn't give me the bayonet. "I promise I'll give it to you when you're older, but if you tell Ma about it now, she'll take it away and you'll never get it," he said.

And that decided it. I'd just have to be patient.

I completely forgot about it after a couple of days, but that was in the box that Brian brought me on my fifteenth birthday. He hadn't forgotten. He left in such a rush on my birthday I didn't get a chance to open it in front of him. It's too bad, too. I think he would've liked to see me open it. Later that night, though, after I'd helped Ma into bed, I took the box into our room and unwrapped it on the bed.

When I took the blade out of the box, I stared at it for a long time. I wondered what it meant.

"So why did you decide to give this to me now? Am I finally *ready*?" I asked sarcastically. Brian didn't smile or laugh at my joke, though. He looked distracted.

"I actually should've given this to you years ago, but I sort of forgot about it," he said. Brian put the bayonet back on the shelf and stared at it for a moment in silence.

"Last time I snuck in here to get my clothes, I came across it in the back of my dresser drawer, stuffed into a sock. I looked at it for a long time. I thought about how I took it so I could protect you. I'm not protecting you anymore. I'm not doing anything for you. I'm just your worthless brother who ran out and left you to take care of our sick mother. I'm not taking care of anything or anyone. But you are. So it's yours."

I shook my head. "You didn't run out on me. Ma doesn't make it easy for you —"

"That doesn't matter," he interrupted. "Ma doesn't make it easy on you either, but you're still here." Brian looked down. "Ma's right, ya' know. I keep fucking up everyone's lives. I fucked up Ma's life with Dan. I fucked up Shannon's life. She's supposed to go out with some smart college guy with a future, instead of letting me sneak into her basement every night."

He stopped and took a breath. He picked his head up and stared blankly ahead, like he was looking at something in his mind's eye instead of what was in front of him.

"I know I should break up with her and let her go off and have a good life, but I just can't let her go. She's the only person in the world who thinks I'm good — like I'm worth something," he said.

"That's not true. Even though she's mad at you, Ma knows you're a good person," I said. I paused for a moment. "And so do I."

Brian turned and looked at me. His face was red. "Poor Nate. I fucked up your life by ditching you and leaving you to take care of everything when you could be kicking ass at school and getting yourself into college…" He swallowed hard. He put his hand over his face and turned away from me. He stood there for a few moments. After a minute, he got control of himself.

We were silent for a few minutes. I just stared at Brian's back, wondering what to say.

"Does Ma know you're here?" I finally said as I

rolled onto my back.

"Nope. I don't feel like fighting with her," Brian said. He fell back on his bed. "I snuck in through the emergency entrance." He nodded toward the open window.

"Can you close that? It's freezing in here."

"Let's sneak out this way. We can hang out. The sun will be up soon. I'll pick up Shannon and we can go down to the water or something," he said, wiping his eyes with the back of his hand.

Fifteen minutes later, after I'd checked on Ma and left a plate of toast and scrambled eggs on her nightstand, Brian and I were cruising in his pickup toward Shannon's house.

"Can we go there? Don't her parents hate you? When do they get home?" I asked.

"They're still up at the resort." He meant Wilton Heights. That was the resort where both of Shannon's parents worked. So a few times a year, they got a free room and they would go stay up there. Shannon's dad was the head of maintenance now. He was a burly, red-faced man who could fix anything, according to Shannon. Shannon's mother was a mousy little blonde woman who managed the housekeeping department. They were hard-working people, but they always pushed Shannon to do well in school. They wanted her to go to college so she wouldn't have to work at the resort when she got older.

"They're coming back tonight. But I actually got to sleep in a bed last night. First time in a month," Brian said.

All of a sudden, I felt the truck slow down. We were still ten houses away from Shannon's. I looked over at Brian to see what was up. He was squinting at something through the windshield.

"Is that who I think it is?" he mumbled.

I looked down at Shannon's house. It was hard to see in the haze of the early morning. Shannon was standing on the porch, holding on to the railing, and standing at the bottom of the stairs was a burly teenage boy. Even from the back, I knew it was Joe Runnel.

"Fuck," I muttered.

"Let's see what's going on," Brian said.

"Nothing's going on, Bri. They're just talking." I looked at Brian when I said it. I could tell he wasn't listening. His eyes were slits as he watched Shannon and Joe.

Suddenly Brian punched the accelerator and we sped down the block. We came to a screeching halt in front of Shannon's house. Shannon looked up and Joe Runnel spun around. His eye was almost completely swollen shut. It took Joe about one second to recognize Brian's truck. He took off and ran between the houses. I almost started to laugh watching him run like that, but I looked back at Brian and he was glaring at Shannon. I could tell there was nothing to laugh at anymore.

Brian got out of the car like a maniac. He was walking toward Shannon like he was gonna tackle her. I got out of the car and ran to catch up.

"Relax, Bri." I put a hand on his shoulder. He shrugged it off and stopped at the stairs, where Joe Runnel had been standing a minute before.

"Baby, it's not what it looks like," Shannon began. "He just came here to apologize for coming to the party." Shannon smiled, trying to lighten the mood. "He sure looked awful sorry, didn't he?"

I laughed, but I could see Brian wasn't buying it.

"Why don't you come inside, Nathan? Bring your brother if he'll come," she said and turned to go back into the house.

I went up the stairs. After a second's hesitation, I could hear Brian's footsteps behind me. I looked around the living room and into the kitchen. Shannon had cleaned up the rest of the mess. You would never have known there'd been a party in her house a few hours earlier. I couldn't even smell the cigarette or pot smoke.

"It looks perfect in here," I said. Brian was still behind me.

"Thanks," Shannon said. "There's still a little bit more to do in the basement, but I'll have it completely clean by the time my parents get back."

"C'mon. I'll help you finish down there," I said.

Shannon and I went down and immediately got busy picking up cups and bottles. Brian followed us a few seconds later. He just stood at the bottom of the stairs, staring at Shannon while she bounced around the basement, taking no notice.

"Are you fucking him?" Brian said.

"That's a nice thing to ask somebody," Shannon said, still cleaning.

"Well?" Brian pressed.

Shannon stopped and turned toward him. She put one hand on her hip and held an empty bottle in the other. "No, baby. I explained this to you two minutes ago. Nothing's going on with him."

"With him? What do you mean? Are there others?" Brian said quickly.

Shannon sighed. "Oh, my God, Brian. I'm so sick of this." She turned toward him and put one hand up like she was taking an oath in court. She said, "I, Shannon Elizabeth Carter, swear to tell the truth, the whole truth, and nothing but the truth, so help me God, that I'm not seeing or fucking anybody except Brian William Keller."

Brian didn't say anything, but his shoulders relaxed a little.

Then, as Shannon turned away from him, she sighed and muttered, "Jesus! I probably should be."

Brian moved so quickly that I didn't even react. He was on Shannon in a second. He grabbed at her arms and I heard him grunt, "You think this is a joke?"

Shannon tried to back away but she was too slow. She flailed her arms wildly to get them free from Brian's grip. Finally, my limbs responded to my brain and I grabbed Brian from behind. He hit me full in the face with his elbow and I was launched backward. The backs of my legs hit the coffee table and I tumbled over it. My head smacked against the concrete floor.

I pushed myself up, but I was seeing black spots in front of me. I staggered to my feet and turned until I could finally see Shannon and Brian again. Shannon was holding a hammer with both hands. She must have picked it up off her dad's workbench. She was backing away from Brian. Every time he crouched toward her, she tensed, ready to swing. She took one hand off the hammer in order to brush the hair out of her face and quickly replaced it. I could see the hammer shaking in her hands.

I tried to get to Brian, but I bumped the coffee table again and stumbled. Suddenly he rushed at her. She brought the hammer down on his shoulder and I heard Brian yell. Then they were both struggling for the hammer. Shannon gained control of it for a second and hit Brian's jaw. But it was only a glancing blow. They were too close to each other.

Enraged, Brian got hold of the hammer and brought it up over his head and down like lightning. I heard a sickening crack, and Shannon fell to the floor. Brian raised the hammer and brought it down on her again.

I finally got to my feet and grabbed Brian from behind. I held him by the shoulders as tightly as I could. I screamed, "Stop, stop! You hurt her!"

Brian raised his arms and shoved me off. He fired the hammer at the floor. It bounced and came to a stop across the room.

"Brian, stop!"

I was watching his back. He was still taking short, fierce breaths, but they started to come more slowly. He was staring down at Shannon's body. I couldn't bring myself to look at her.

All of sudden, Brian shuddered. His broad shoulders seemed to shrink. As his rage left him, his whole body seemed to deflate. He leaned down to look more closely at Shannon. When he finally spoke, his voice was barely above a whisper.

"Oh, my God."

I finally looked down at Shannon's face. Her mouth was open, like she was sleeping soundly, but her eyes were open, too. The soft sparkle in her eyes, the one that lit up her whole face, was gone. Her eyes were vacant—they looked like glass. And her golden hair was crusted with blood. There was a gash and a smear of red across her forehead. A dark stain was slowly spreading across the gray concrete of the basement floor beneath her.

I knew Shannon was dead.

Chapter Four

As I approached the parking lot at the beach, I slowed down. Before I turned into it, I wanted to make sure there were no other cars there. There weren't. As the tires hit the gravel, the truck lurched, and Brian's body swayed along with it. It was like he had no control over himself anymore. He hadn't said a word since I'd pushed him into the truck and sped away from Shannon's.

I got out and ran around to the passenger door. Brian still hadn't moved. His blue eyes were vacant as I opened the door and pulled him out of the truck. He was staring out at the water, seeing nothing. I turned for a moment to look and the water was electric. Choppy white caps writhed along the surface and the wind blew the salty spray onto the shore. Summer was almost over.

I yanked on Brian's arm and he still didn't

49

move. I put my shoulder under his arm and started to drag him up the path. He began to walk with me in shuffling steps.

"C'mon. We've got to find the cave," I said in his ear.

"Where are we going, Nate?" Brian said thickly.

"There's a cave off the path up here. Dylan told me about it. He and Maggie go there to smoke weed and fuck during the summertime," I said. "No one will be there now. You'll be safe there, Bri."

"I killed her, Nate. I killed her."

"I know. You've gotta help me out here. We've gotta get you somewhere they won't find you."

Brian looked down at me, struggling under his arm. "You're a good brother, Nathan." He almost never called me Nathan. Brian reached out his big hand and patted the top of my head. I saw that his hand was still covered in Shannon's blood. So did he. Brian stopped abruptly and began to sob.

When Brian stopped, I lost my balance and fell face-first into the cold, wet sand. I rolled over onto my back and looked up at my older brother. Around the hand that Brian had placed over his face, I could see the blush and tears on his cheeks. I laid my head back and sighed.

"What the hell happened?" Brian spat between sobs. "I don't know what happened."

"You went fucking crazy again. That's what happened." I'd said it more to myself than anything, but Brian had heard me.

"I'm not crazy. I don't know what happens. People start with me and suddenly everything spins out of control." For a second, I thought his anger was giving him focus, purpose. I figured at least now he might start following me without me having to drag him down the path. All of a sudden, he started sobbing again. "They're gonna put me away for this. Oh, my God. I killed her. I killed Shannon!" After that, his sobs became so muddled I couldn't tell what he was saying.

He was crying so hard that he started coughing. I stood up and slapped him on the back to help him get it out. Brian fell to his knees and vomited in the sand.

"Great. Just great," I said under my breath.

"Shut up!" Brian said. He wiped his mouth with the back of his hand and then he put his head down in the sand.

"C'mon, Bri. We can't talk about it here. We've got to go a little farther up the path."

I started up the path. Brian followed. No more heaving. No more sobs. I walked slowly, paying attention to the wear on the path and looking near the ground. Suddenly, there was a shadowy opening in the rock wall. I knelt down and looked inside. Dylan said that the entrance was small and that we'd have to crawl to get in. I crawled in.

"Nate, what are you doing?"

"I think this is the cave," I said quietly. It was almost completely dark. The small entrance didn't allow much light in. I crawled straight ahead from the cave mouth, feeling around in the darkness. Finally, my hand came to rest on a piece of smooth plastic. I pressed down and the cave lit up. When I looked down, I saw that my hand was resting on the small battery-powered light that Dylan had told me about. This was the place.

Brian was a lot bigger than me, so he had some trouble getting through the mouth of the cave. Once he'd gotten his shoulders through, he had to shimmy the rest of his body in to the narrow opening.

Once we were inside, we realized we could stand in the cave. In fact, the inside of the cave was actually really big. In one corner, there was a bunch of balled-up food wrappers. Right near the entrance were a few crushed Old Style beer cans.

"This is cool," I said.

"I can't believe how smooth the sand is in

here," Brian said.

"I guess that Dylan cleaned up all the glass shards and cigarette butts before they did it on the floor," I said.

Brian snorted out a short laugh. It was the closest thing to a normal sound I'd heard out of him since we left Shannon's.

"This is a good spot, little bro," he said.

"Yeah, it's pretty big in here, plus you've got the light. And since the entrance is so small, no one will come looking in here."

"What about Dylan?" Brian rubbed his chin.

"Don't worry about him. Maggie said it's too cold to do it out here anymore this year. They'll just do it in the car," I said.

Brian smirked. The smirk quickly left his face.

"So what's gonna happen now, Nate?"

"I don't know. The cops will come looking for you. Probably Marisconi. It seems like they always send him. It's like he's our own personal cop," I said.

"I hate that fucking pig," Brian hissed.

"Me too. But it'll probably be him. When her parents find her, they'll call the cops and then Marisconi will come and ask me and Ma where you are. And we'll say we don't know."

"Will Ma go along with that? I mean…I can usually count on Ma. She's never let Marisconi get me before. She's always stood up for me, but she's just been so pissed at me lately…" Brian said.

"Bri, she's mad at you right now, sure. But she's been protecting you your whole life. And besides, I'm not gonna tell her that I know where you are. So when she says she doesn't know, she'll be telling the truth. I don't wanna get Ma in trouble. The less she knows, the better."

"Yeah. I guess you're right. But she probably already knows you're gone, man. She always looks in our room at night when she gets up to pee," Brian said.

I shook my head. "Naw, I doubt it. She hasn't been able to get up that much the last few days. She pissed the bed yesterday. I had to help her into the chair and change the sheets and then her clothes. She's really out of it."

Brian didn't say anything for a few seconds. After a while, I wasn't sure he'd heard me at all. His mind was already somewhere else.

"Should we have left the house like that? We just left Shannon there on the floor. We wrecked the house," Brian said. His voice was small. He sounded like a little kid—a scared little kid.

"I don't know, Bri. I'm not sure what we're

54

doing."

Brian stared at me with his glassy blue eyes. After a few seconds, I couldn't stand him staring at me anymore. I looked down.

"I'm sorry, Nate."

I still couldn't look at him. "Yeah. I know."

When I finally looked up at him, Brian had covered his face again and was sobbing silently.

I turned toward the entrance of the cave and said over my shoulder, "I better get going. I'll get you some supplies and then I'm going home. You got your phone in case I need to call you?"

"No," he said huskily. I could tell he was still crying. "I left it at Shannon's."

"Okay." I needed to get out of there.

I crawled out of the cave and headed back up the path toward the parking lot. I dug into my pockets and found a few dollars. It wasn't much, but it would get Brian through today. I'd have to get some more money for supplies right away. I didn't know how I was going to do that.

Before I walked out from the path and into the parking lot, I stopped and peered around. I wanted to make sure no one else was here or had seen where Brian was hidden. Even if they didn't know us, or what Brian had done, we'd look suspicious enough for most people to notice. I didn't see any cars in the lot or any people out yet. It was still early.

I ran across the lot to Brian's truck and got moving. I got off Beach Street as soon as I could. There wasn't anyone out yet, but Beach was just too busy. There was too much of a chance someone would see Brian's truck and recognize it. So I turned off onto Old Mill Road and drove quickly back toward town. I still didn't know what the hell I was going to do with Brian's truck.

I was just about to turn and find a place to stow the truck on the north end of town when I saw it—Grayson's Garage. It'd been abandoned for years and no one ever bought it or rented it to try and start another mechanic's shop. I pulled up to the garage door on the far left of the building because I could see that it was open a little. I got out and pulled up hard on the garage door. It slowly creaked to life and after much sweating and swearing, I got it open enough to fit the truck.

I pulled the truck into the garage and then I had to pull myself up on the open door and let my body weight pull the rusty door closed. It wasn't the best or the safest place to hide the truck, but I didn't know what else to do.

I went through the garage, looking for stuff that might help Brian. I found a bunch of blankets. They were really dusty and most of them were covered in grease. I'd seen mechanics at the resort put blankets on the exteriors of cars and boats while they worked on them in order to avoid scrapes or oil stains. I picked out the two cleanest ones I could find. I figured Brian would need them for the cold nights in the cave.

From then on, I was on foot. I actually felt better, just walking back toward the store. It was normal. I walked a lot of places around town, even though Ma said I could use the van whenever I wanted. I don't have a license yet, so I try not to use it too much in case I get caught. It might get Ma in trouble. Although every time I tell her that, she says, "You tell any cop who tries to bust you that your mother whose got cancer needs you to drive around and run errands for her. That'd make any cop ashamed for bringing you in." I'm not so sure she's right about that, so I try not to drive too much.

I went into the gas station convenience store off Eighth Street, Jed's. I hardly ever go in there because it's dirty and everything you buy there smells like exhaust. Brian was just going to have to live with that for now.

I knew if I went to the store down on Ocean Boulevard next to Maltby's, Oceanview Grocery, the owner or his wife might recognize me. I often bought myself a soda there before work. So I figured

I'd better steer clear of Oceanview, even though it was a hell of a lot closer to the beach than Jed's. I bought Brian some chips, sodas, and a couple of sub sandwiches wrapped in cellophane. The clerk, a rail-thin freak with a seventies mustache, didn't say anything to me as he put them in a paper bag.

As I walked back toward the beach, there were more people out. Just a block from the convenience store, I walked past an old man working on a blue Chevy in his driveway. I nodded at him as I passed. He raised one hand in greeting. It looked like he was about to say something, but I quickly turned away and walked past his house. A few cars passed me as I tried to walk casually back toward the beach with my blankets and my "lunch," in case anybody asked.

When I got to the beach, there was a black Honda in the parking lot. I didn't see anyone in it. As I headed up the path, I could hear voices up ahead. There were already people playing volleyball on the beach. I didn't want these people to see me, but at the same time I didn't want to walk away suspiciously. I stopped near the mouth of the cave and I dropped the bag and the blankets in front of it. I tried to make it look casual, like I was just dropping trash on the beach like everyone else. I waited there for a few seconds, and suddenly a hand shot out, grabbed the bag, and pulled it in to the cave. The hand shot back out and pulled the blankets in, too.

I could hear the rustling of the bag. Suddenly, the hand shot out again and gave me a thumbs-up.

I walked back to our house as fast as I could. I needed to get some sleep before it all came down.

CHAPTER FIVE

Sleep came as soon as I hit the pillow. It seemed like minutes later when I heard my mother, her voice straining from the next room. "Nate! Nate! Get up!"

I opened my eyes and rolled over onto my back. The room was full of alternating bands of sunlight and shade from the blinds. It was late afternoon. I looked over at Brian's bed. It was empty, of course. I couldn't remember the last time he slept in it. The sheets were twisted and the cereal box was still next to his pillow.

I pushed myself up from the bed and put on my jeans. I walked through the house with my eyes half-closed. When I got to my mother's door, I rubbed the sleep out of them. I pushed it open and searched for her in the darkness. She has drapes over her blinds. She tries to keep out as much light as possible.

"Jesus, Nathan. It took you long enough."

I spoke into the darkness while my eyes adjusted. "You need something, Ma?"

"Is today the day for my treatment?" she asked thickly.

"No, Ma. That was Thursday morning. Two days ago. You don't remember?" I pushed my hair to the back of my head. Sometimes I think the chemo has messed her up more than the cancer.

"Of course I do," she said. "Can you get my cigarettes from the dresser?"

"Ma, they aren't helping you," I said. I brought her the pack of Winstons and the red lighter from the dresser.

"Shut up, Nathan," she said with a cigarette dangling from her mouth. She fumbled with the lighter.

"Give me this. You're going to burn the fucking house down." I took the lighter from her and guided her head forward to light the cigarette. Her face was thin. What's that word, gaunt? I think that's it. She has the same glassy blue eyes as Brian, but hers are sunken in.

She took a long drag and blew the smoke out in front of her. "Watch your mouth," she said.

"Sorry. I don't even notice I'm saying it."

She dropped it and asked the same question she asks me every morning. "Have you seen your brother?"

I lied. "Not since he came here on my birthday."

"If you see him, tell your brother he should visit his sick mother," she said.

"Yeah, okay, Ma." Considering the last time Ma saw him she pretty much called Brian a fucking disgrace, I probably wouldn't have relayed that message even under normal circumstances.

"You need something, Ma?" I had to ask things twice a lot lately.

"I'm hungry and I want to watch TV," she said.

I got her out of the bed, put her on the rolling desk chair from my room, and rolled her out to the living room. I maneuvered the chair around the big potted fern and stopped in front of our worn gray couch. I lifted her and pushed the chair out of the way before letting her fall onto the cushions. When I lifted her, her bony arms tightened a little around my neck, but she wasn't strong enough to hold on.

I sat her up and she reached up and touched my face. "You're a good son."

I didn't look at her. I dropped her cigarettes and the lighter on the grainy old coffee table.

"Yeah, Ma. I'll make you something to eat."

"No. Really. You've taken wonderful care of me, Nathan. Are you looking out for Brian, too? Now that I'm sick, I can't do it," she said as she tried to push herself farther up on the couch.

I stopped in the kitchen and stood there with my back to her. I could feel her watching me. Finally, I turned around. "Yeah, Ma. I'm doing the best I can to keep him out of trouble." I sighed and turned back into the kitchen.

"Are you sure?" she asked.

"Yeah, Ma. I'm sure." I couldn't look at her.

She didn't say anything for a few seconds. It felt like she was thinking, trying to choose the right thing to say next. She must've given up. All she said was, "Close the shades, will you?"

I heated up some soup out of a can for Ma and fed it to her. She couldn't hold the spoon on her own. She only ate a few mouthfuls before she leaned back against the couch cushions.

"I'm full, honey," was all she said. I knew she needed to eat more, but I was too tired to argue with her.

I cleaned up and started washing the dishes. Out of all the chores I do in the house, this is the only one I don't mind. The sound of the water running is peaceful. It gives me a chance to think.

Except this time, as I stood at the sink, all I kept thinking about was Shannon. I replayed that moment over and over again, where Brian brought the hammer down on her. I heard the cracking sound like it was right in my ears. I'm glad Ma wasn't paying attention because I'm sure I flinched even as I thought about it.

I could still see the emptiness in that beautiful face and how dark Shannon's blood was as it stained the basement floor. I'd never seen that much blood before.

I also remembered the position of her body. She had fallen in a heap and her arm had been bent badly as it was pinned beneath her. If she were alive, that would've been extremely painful. Her arm might have been broken—I don't know.

I guess it didn't matter, but for one brief moment I'd wanted to reach out and pull her arm out from under her. I just wanted to make her comfortable. It's crazy, I know. I didn't touch her.

Suddenly, a sharp knock at the door brought me back to reality.

I jumped at the sound at first, but then I realized that this had to happen sooner or later. I looked over at Ma to see if she noticed. She was dozing on the couch.

"Ellen, open the door." The light from the

window on the door was blocked out by Detective Marisconi's big head.

I walked over slowly and opened it.

Marisconi pushed past me and walked into the house. He's been here plenty of times before. Frank Marisconi is the senior detective in Wilton and a drunk. He's been coming here since he was a regular uniformed cop dealing with all of Brian and Ma's shit. He was unshaven, as usual. He was wearing a white shirt with a solid red tie. He held his jacket over his shoulder like he was Frank fucking Sinatra.

"I've got to talk to Brian," he said.

"He's not here."

"I had a feeling," Marisconi said.

Marisconi looked down at my mother. There was drool dripping from the side of her mouth. I reached down and wiped it off with my thumb.

"Wake her up," he barked.

I whispered back at him. "She's out of it. The treatments are really messing her up. She needs to sleep."

"Do it."

I looked at him hard. He stared right back. There's usually a tired glaze over his eyes. I figure it's a combination of his boredom from dealing with us, and booze. But this morning—no boredom.

I squatted down and gently squeezed her shoulder. "Ma, you gotta wake up. Marisconi's here."

Her eyelids fluttered, but they didn't open. I was staring at the smear of blue between her eyebrows and the sockets when Marisconi suddenly lunged forward and kneed me out of the way. I fell backward and landed on my butt.

"Jesus Christ! I don't have time for this." Marisconi dropped his jacket on the arm of the couch and reached over Ma's head. He yanked down the string that opens the blinds. Suddenly, the sharp sunlight poured in through the window.

"C'mon, Ellen! You gotta wake up," he barked. He reached down to shake her when I jumped to my feet. I was on him before his hand got there. I pushed him away from her with both hands. He outweighs me by about fifty pounds, but I still managed to get him moving backward and falling off balance. Once he was away from my mother, I threw a haymaker at him from about three feet away.

"Don't you touch her!"

I missed. Marisconi grabbed my arm as it went by and before I knew it, I was facedown on the carpet, my arm pinned behind me. Marisconi put his knee on my arm and leaned on me. It felt like my arm was about to snap.

Marisconi leaned down so close to me I could smell the coffee on his breath when he spoke. "All of a sudden you're a tough guy like your brother, huh?"

"Get offa him!" Ma yelled. She couldn't get up, but she waved her stick arms and tried to grab at Marisconi from the couch.

Marisconi leaned forward and I felt a throbbing pain in my elbow. Then, he leaned back slowly.

"I'm gonna let you up, so take it easy, tough guy," Marisconi said. He waited another few seconds before quickly standing up and backing away from me.

Out of breath, I rolled over onto my back and rubbed my arm. The whole arm hurt, from the shoulder all the way down. I bent my elbow back and forth to make sure it still worked.

"You come here to rough up my other boy now?" Ma said. I looked up at her and she leaned back on the couch. The effort of yelling at Marisconi and trying to grab at him really took it out of her. She was exhausted.

"Ellen, listen, this isn't about Nathan. It's about Brian," he said.

"What now?" Ma said.

"Shannon Carter is dead, Ellen. She was beaten to death with a hammer."

Ma pulled in her chin but didn't say anything.

"I need to talk to Brian," Marisconi said.

"Why? You don't think he was involved in anything like that? He loved that girl." It seemed to hit Ma all at once. "Oh, my God — this is gonna kill him. That girl was the one good thing he had going…" — Ma paused to take a deep breath. I could tell she was trying to fight back a sob. She finally got control of herself and finished — "going for him in his whole life."

"Oh, cut the goddamned sob story," Marisconi said. "Tell me where he is."

Ma sat up just a little. Her eyes were slits as she peered at the cop. "Not here. I don't know where he is. And I wouldn't tell you if I knew."

"Watch it, Ellen." Marisconi pointed a thick finger at my mother.

They stared at each other for a few seconds. Finally, Marisconi let out a breath as I got to my feet.

"What about you, Sport-o?" He was still looking at my mother when he asked me the question.

"I don't know where he is," I said. "He didn't sleep here last night."

"I'm gonna go check his room." Marisconi

turned and walked out of the living room and through the kitchen to the bedroom in the back of the house.

While Marisconi was in the bedroom, Ma and I didn't speak, but she stared at me, searching my eyes to see if there was anything I wasn't telling her. I tried to keep my face from moving. I tried to make it totally blank.

Marisconi's heavy footsteps got louder. He was back in the living room, standing over Ma.

"When's the last time you saw him?" he said.

"I dunno. A couple a days," Ma said.

"You, Sport-o?" He turned toward me. I was as tall as he was. He was really close to me. I could see the pockmarks in his face beneath the raw stubble.

"Wednesday, maybe?" I tried to sound casual, like it was no big deal.

"Where were you last night?" he said immediately. He could tell something was up.

"Working at Maltby's, and then I was here. I had homework," I said.

"That's right. The schoolboy." Marisconi paused. I could tell he was thinking about what he was gonna say next.

He finally spit it out. "What kinda homework?"

"Chemistry. I'm writing a lab report," I said. It came out smoothly. I'd already played out this scenario in my head. I thought about what Marisconi would ask me and how I would answer. He wasn't gonna get me.

"You do homework on Friday night?" he asked.

I shrugged. "It's Saturday. I gotta work today and tomorrow. When else am I supposed to do it?"

"Do you think your brother killed her?" he asked me.

"Hell, no," I said right away. "Brian's got problems, but Ma's right. He loves Shannon. He wouldn't hurt her."

Marisconi pointed at me. "Your brother, who once beat up a kid at school so bad that he was in the hospital for a week. He couldn't have done nothing like that? C'mon, Nate. We both know there's something wrong with him."

I shook my head but Marisconi just kept going.

"Remember that time your ma called us and I got here just in time. Remember, Brian was kneeling on your chest and holding a piece of broken glass to your throat in the yard. He was screaming that he was gonna kill you. It took both me and your stepdad—what the hell was that guy's name?"

My mother answered him. "Dan Howe."

"That's right, Dan Howe. It took both me and Dan to get him offa you—he went so fucking crazy. And you don't think he could hurt someone he cares about?" He stared at me like he was waiting for an answer.

I was determined not to tell him anything. I was still shaking my head, but I could feel tears welling up in my eyes. I don't even remember what I did to make Brian so mad that time. My cheeks must've been bright red.

"All right, Frank. For Christ's sake, leave him alone," Ma said.

Marisconi turned to my mother. "I'm just saying, Ellen. The kid's got a history. What if he found out that Shannon was cheating on him with some other guy? What if she told him she was gonna break up with him? You don't think he'd go crazy?"

If I'd been red before, I must've turned white when he said that. As Marisconi talked, I started to shake. He might be an asshole and a drunk, but Marisconi's got a brain. He figured pretty close to what happened on the first try. I was glad he wasn't looking at me right then.

"I gotta talk to him," Marisconi said.

"We'll tell him if we see him," Ma said.

My head was down, but I could feel Marisconi's stare on me. "Anything you wanna tell me, Sport-o?"

I shook my head.

He put his hand under my chin and lifted up my face. "Nathan, you know something."

71

I lowered my head and shook it again. He put his hand on my shoulder, like he was trying to be fatherly or something.

"I'm gonna find him, Nate. There's no doubt. It'll be a lot easier on him if he just comes forward."

I shook my head again. Marisconi took his hand off my shoulder. I tried to raise my eyes up and look at him. I didn't want him to think I was scared.

When I did raise my eyes, Marisconi wasn't looking at me. He was looking at his hand—the one he'd just taken off my shoulder. He rubbed his index finger and thumb together. I could see the little grains of sand fall from his fingertips to the carpet.

Shit.

Chapter Six

After Marisconi left, I paced back and forth in my room for a while, wondering what I was going to do.

I knew it wouldn't be safe to go see Brian for a little while. Marisconi probably wouldn't find Brian in the cave, but he would definitely have someone watching over the beach the next couple of days. I also knew he'd have someone watching me to see if I'd go back there and lead him right to Brian.

I picked up my phone and I was about to call Brian to warn him that there might be cops around the beach, but then I remembered that he'd left his phone at Shannon's.

There was nothing I could do but wait it out, so I started to think about things I could bring Brian the next time I went to the beach. I knew he could probably use a sleeping bag. We used to have one, but I didn't know where it was anymore. Brian had a little food. If he didn't eat everything right away, he'd make it the two days until Monday. With Marisconi on the lookout, he'd have to. I knew he needed more supplies. I could grab some cans of food out of the pantry. Ma wouldn't miss them. But Brian needed more than that. The problem was I didn't have any more money.

When Ma fell asleep on the couch that night, I went through her whole dresser looking for cash. I didn't find much. I came across a few singles and a cash station receipt showing that her account only had $17.04 left in it. I was crouched down, staring at the receipt, when I heard her call me from the couch.

"What are you looking for?" she asked. She wheezed a little when she said it.

I came out into the living room. Ma was slumped on the couch. Her body looked smaller than I'd ever seen it. Her hands were at her sides, palms up. I wasn't even sure she could move them.

"Nothing, Ma. Don't worry about it."

"Do you need money for Brian?" she asked.

I shook my head. I didn't want to get her involved in this.

"Yes, you do," she said. She lifted her hand and held out her debit card to me. "Take it. Take what you need. You know the code."

"No, Ma. It's okay." I didn't want to tell her that I'd seen the receipt. I didn't want to tell her that you can't even get $17 out of an ATM.

I guess I didn't realize how bad things were with money since Ma hasn't been able to work. And she'd kept that a secret from me. Even when she was dying, she was trying to keep me from worrying. Or maybe she didn't even remember. I don't know which possibility made me feel worse.

My eyes suddenly stung. I looked down.

"Nathan, I know you're helping Brian. It's okay. I want to help you help him," she said.

I put my hand over my eyes and shook my head again. "You can't, Ma."

"I took care of that boy his entire life. I made sure they never put him away or sent him off to some therapy camp." Ma's voice dripped with anger. "Brian's not crazy. Everyone thinks he is, but he's not."

"He did a real bad thing, Ma."

"How do you know he even did it?" she asked immediately. "Marisconi, his teachers, and that principal at your school used to make up shit about your brother all the time. He gets angry sometimes, but he'd never really harm anyone."

I couldn't even look at her. Even now, she

didn't understand Brian or what he had done. Someone who loved him, imperfectly maybe, but someone who loved him was dead because he couldn't control himself. I always wanted to be like Ma and believe that Brian wasn't capable of anything really terrible. But now…

I turned and ran to my room. I could hear her calling after me. "Nathan! Nathan you get back here!"

I knew I'd have to get the money some other way.

That some other way came the next night, Sunday, while I was working at Maltby's. It was me and Dylan again, playing our usual roles. I did all the work while he talked to customers, gave cute girls free cones, and at the end of the night, Dylan left with Maggie only minutes after we closed. And lucky for me, he didn't cash out his register.

I went through the cash and receipts. It had been a pretty good night. I figured it would be pretty easy to eliminate a few receipts and take about $30 off the top of the cash. That'd be enough to buy Brian a bunch of cans of food and other stuff. He could stay hidden for a while until we figured out what he was gonna do.

I went through the receipts and picked random ones to eliminate until I had what I needed.

I figured I couldn't take too much. Mr. Harris, the owner, might notice from the stock of cups, cones, and what was left in the ice cream buckets that he was missing cash if it was any more than that.

After I got the money for Brian, I put the remaining cash and receipts in the envelope, filled out the information on the front, and put it in the safe. I figured I could go to the store after school on Monday and then sneak out to the cave. Brian would definitely be out of food by then.

I didn't want to go to school on Monday, but I figured I would have to make like everything was normal, or else Marisconi would become suspicious and have the entire department on the lookout for me. I figured he'd probably already contacted the school and asked them to keep tabs on my attendance. I only knew about this because Marisconi would always check Brian's attendance when he was investigating something that he thought Brian might be involved in.

Wilton High was one of the biggest buildings in town. It was just a couple of blocks from downtown, in a residential area right near the beach. It was just a couple of blocks north of our house. The building was richly decorated brick and stone. There were Roman columns at the front and gargoyles on the highest corners. The building was around sixty years old and had been built when the fishing and resort industries were booming back in the 1950s. It was dark and rundown now, but it was still a sight to behold.

I'll never forget one time our cousins were visiting over the summer from DC. I was eight or nine. Tommy was a year older than me and we had been riding bikes through the neighborhood near the beach. When we came to the school, Tommy stopped in front of it and just stared at the dark and forbidding building. He asked me what it was. I told him it was the high school. He said it looked like the prison they'd passed in Arlandria on the way up to visit us.

At the time, I remember being offended by that. Now I'm not so sure it was off the mark.

That morning I got to school just before the first bell rang. I walked slowly and I tried not to look at anyone. It took me a while to realize that no one had spoken to me all the way up to the third floor where my locker was. I'm not a popular kid. I'm just a nothing sophomore, but I know enough kids that I should've passed someone who yelled, "Hey, Nate."

As I was standing in front of my open locker, I looked down the hall to my left. There were a bunch of kids staring at me. A few were whispering to each other. I guess I should've seen that coming. Word was bound to get out about Shannon. I just didn't think that word about Brian would get out so quickly.

Most people looked away when I made eye contact with them, but a few kept staring at me. There was one guy wearing a San Francisco 49ers jersey who nodded at me while I stared him down.

I usually don't like to start trouble. My goal in school is usually to read something interesting and blend in to the walls, but I didn't like the way this kid was looking at me.

"You got a problem?" I said quietly to him from across the hall. All the chatter around us stopped. It was as if everyone around was waiting to see if something was gonna happen with me.

"No. No problem, Keller," the kid said. He had dark eyebrows that almost met above the bridge of his nose.

"How do you know my name?" I said.

"Everybody knows you. You're the psycho-killer's little brother," he said. A boy standing next to him actually laughed.

I didn't know what to do. I didn't want to fight. I just wanted to be left alone.

"Yeah, okay," I said and turned back to my locker.

"Did he kill her? Shannon Carter?" the kid said from across the hall.

I tried to pretend I couldn't hear him. I tried to pretend he wasn't there.

"He bashed her brains in with a hammer, right? Like this — *bam!*" he yelled at me.

Out of the corner of my eye, I saw a freshman girl wince when the kid made the pounding motion. Then I could hear whispers, chatter, and footsteps coming toward me. The kid was coming up behind me. I turned around and faced him.

"I don't want any trouble," I said. "And my brother didn't do anything."

"That's not what I heard," he said. "Joe Runnel said he was talking to her early in the morning after her party and then your brother shows up and the next thing we know, she's dead."

"I heard the house was robbed," I said. I just wanted this kid to get away from me. My stomach was churning. I felt like I might throw up any second.

"Is there a problem here?" Mr. Vancil, one of the PE teachers, had just turned down the hall. He came up and stopped next to the kid with a million questions. Mr. Vancil was a lean former army sergeant. Nobody messed with him.

The kid looked me up and down. "No. There

ain't no problem here," he said, turning away.

Mr. Vancil stood there staring at me. I could tell by the way he was looking at me he knew what was going on. I bet the teachers had already had a meeting that morning. Everyone knew what was going on. "Get to class, kid," he finally said.

I turned back to my locker and grabbed some books—I didn't even care if they were the right ones. Then I walked as fast as I could without running toward my first class. I sat in my classes with a blank stare on my face that morning. I tried to look straight ahead. I didn't care what anyone was talking about. I just wanted to become invisible.

I knew lunch would be a dangerous time, so I decided to skip it and go to the library. Nobody would be in there. School had just started, so no teachers would bring their classes up and even the serious students didn't have enough homework to have to work through their lunches just yet.

I slid in the door and went to the cubicles in the back. I figured that would be about as far away from people as I could get. I was wrong. In the last cubicle, there was a skinny Mexican girl leaning on her elbow and doodling in a notebook.

She had dark, wavy hair, and skin that was a radiant color somewhere between chocolate and gold. She hadn't noticed me yet. I could've turned around and slunk off to another corner of the library, but I didn't. I put my books down in the cubicle at the other end of the row.

She looked up at me. I turned toward my cubicle, pulled out the chair, and sat down. I figured she would get the hint I didn't want to talk.

"You're the boy everyone's been talking about," she whispered.

Damn it.

I figured if I said something right away, she might get the point and we could both just sit in silence and get through lunch.

"Yeah. I'm the guy everyone is talking about. And I didn't go to lunch because I didn't want to look at people, and talk to people, and hear them whispering about me, okay? So please don't bother me," I said with as much aggression as I could muster in a whisper.

She was silent for a few minutes. I figured I'd gotten my point across. Suddenly, she said something else. "I haven't gone to lunch in three years."

"You look hungry. Maybe you should go," I said a little louder.

"I probably should," she said. "No one even knows me here. I've got nothing to hide from here." What the hell was she talking about?

All of a sudden, she got up and walked to the cubicle next to mine, pulled out the chair, and sat down. I would've tried to ignore her, but I was so shocked that I just stared at her. She looked like she was about to throw up.

Her eyebrows came together in concentration as she spoke. "When I was in eighth grade back in Michigan, my sister, Ana, killed herself," she said. "She was a senior in high school. She hung herself with a belt that she fastened to the coatrack on her closet door. My mother found her on a Saturday morning. I'll never forget that first day I went back to school after her funeral. All the kids stared at me and whispered. No one could stop looking at me. It felt like I was covered in my sister's blood or something. I skipped lunch to get away from everyone. I never went back. I never understood what I must've looked like that day — until I just saw you."

I was stunned. I just kept staring at her.

"My name is Celia," she said. Her face softened and she tried to smile. She even put out her hand like she wanted me to shake it. I couldn't move.

She put her hand down. "Well, I won't bother you anymore," she said. "I don't know what came over me. I just saw you and all sorts of feelings just hit me. I hope things get better for you and your family." She got up and turned to go back to her cubicle.

"Will I ever feel normal again?" I said.

She turned back toward me. "No. At least I never did. It never gets easier either. People tell you it will, but…"

"But what?"

"But they're wrong. They don't know how it feels," she said.

"Great."

"It never gets easier, but you learn how to deal with it. You learn how to live—and what to live for," she said.

"What do you live for?" I asked.

"My younger sister, Natalia." She smiled when she said the name. "I always want her to have her sister."

As I stared at her, I wondered what I was going to live for when this was all over. I just didn't know.

Chapter Seven

How could I be thinking about a girl right now?

As I sat in geometry class staring at the shapes on the projector screen, I kept seeing Celia's dark eyes with her eyebrows furrowed in concentration as she spoke to me in the library. The sound of her voice was like nothing I'd ever heard before. There was a sort of breathlessness to it. It was as if every word she said was so desperate. It's the same sound my voice makes in my own head. I don't know if I really do it out loud, but I always feel like everyone can tell how desperate I am.

Celia wasn't beautiful, exactly. I know girls hate this, but if someone asked me, I'd probably say she was cute. I remember one time when Brian was telling Ma about a new girl who had moved to town and had just been put in his class. Brian was probably in the seventh grade at the time, and he told Ma that the girl was cute. Ma told Brian never to say that to any girl.

"Girls don't want to be cute," she'd said. "They want to be pretty, attractive, words like that. Otherwise they feel like a puppy or something."

But Celia *was* cute. She was small, skinny. And from what I saw, she wasn't dressed to impress anyone either. She'd been wearing jeans and a yellow T-shirt. She'd looked so distracted before I sat down, too. She reminded me of me. Ma is always telling me that my head is somewhere else.

But I guess Celia wasn't beautiful like Shannon.

Shannon.

I saw her face as she lay lifeless on the basement floor. I forced it out of my mind. I didn't want to think about her like that.

I remember when Brian started bringing her around. I was only like eleven, so I didn't understand why Brian wanted to spend so much time with a girl. I figured it out as I got older.

Shannon was beautiful. There was really no argument to be made about it. She just was. She was sort of the opposite of Celia in a lot of ways. She was tall and had curves in all the right places, even way back when she was in eighth grade. And she had this golden hair. It wasn't blonde—it really was gold. Other people with blonde hair have really light hair that's almost white or sort of darker hair with hints of brown in it. Not Shannon. Her hair looked like the late afternoon sun.

But Shannon wasn't just pretty either. She was always laughing and joking, and she always made people feel like they were important.

I'll never forget when my stepdad, Dan, left my mother. Shannon made Brian bring her to our house. She made dinner for all of us. She even chopped up all the vegetables for the salad herself. She wouldn't let any of us help. After dinner, Brian and I cleaned up while Shannon sat on the couch with Ma.

They spoke quietly. Brian and I couldn't hear what they were saying. Shannon held my mother's hand most of the time. I remember how shocked we were when they both started crying and hugging. Brian went over there to find out if everything was okay. Ma got up and ran in her room. Shannon followed and told us not to come in.

Brian and I finished cleaning up and watched TV awhile, but we both kept glancing at the door to Ma's room. Finally, Brian couldn't take it anymore and we went over and opened the door. Ma had fallen asleep in Shannon's arms. I remember

Shannon holding our mother so gently that she could finally sleep peacefully.

That was the first time I felt something for Shannon. I remember going to bed that night thinking that we were all lucky to have Shannon in our lives. But before I fell asleep that night, I remember thinking about what it would be like to be in Shannon's arms. Of course, I felt terrible for thinking it, but there was a small part of me that thought Brian wasn't good enough for her then. He wasn't gentle or caring enough for her. I was. And I needed her more than he did, anyway.

The next morning I woke up and realized that I was just plain jealous. Even though I was guilty and ashamed, the feelings wouldn't stop, so I did my best to hide them.

But until now, it also made me compare every girl to Shannon. I've never had a real girlfriend. It's not that I don't notice or like girls. Jesus, I notice every girl — their eyes, their hair, their bodies, how they smell, but none of them made me feel the way Shannon did. I don't know…maybe Celia did today.

I almost told Brian about Shannon, the way I felt. It was last year when Brian asked me if I was gay. I could see where he was coming from. I never went out with anyone. Hell, I never even talked about girls. So Brian was just wondering.

I remember looking down at my feet and not knowing what to say. He said, "It's okay, bro. You can tell me. I'm not gonna be mad or disown you or anything." I remember wishing I were gay instead of being in love with Shannon. That would've made things a lot easier. Eventually, I just convinced him that I was really shy, which is pretty much true anyway. For a few weeks after that, Brian introduced me to dozens of girls. It seemed to be his personal mission to get me laid.

It probably would've worked, too, if I'd cooperated. I just kept making up excuses and a couple of times, I even made up stories about girls at school that I was working up my courage to ask out. Since Brian had dropped out, he couldn't interfere there.

Finally, though, Brian got really mad at me and one day when the three of us were hanging out at the beach, he started on me again.

"Do you wanna have sex with trees or something, Nate?" he asked me. "For Chrissake's, you're fifteen. It's not normal!"

Shannon came to my rescue that day, though. Sitting in the sand with a bottle of Coke half filled with Rum, she said to Brian, "Don't you think the reason Nathan is having trouble with girls is that you're putting so much pressure on him?"

When Brian went to swim and Shannon and I were sitting alone on the blanket, I said, "Thanks for getting him off my case."

"No problem. He shouldn't be all over you about this all the time. But do me a favor, don't let him catch you doing it with any trees."

We both laughed about that one.

I always had this feeling that Shannon knew I liked her. A girl like Shannon would be used to that, though. Most guys had feelings for her, even if they were only physical. She never said anything or made me uncomfortable, though. I think she actually used to look at me as cute. You know, like a puppy.

Until I kissed her, of course. I saw it as if it just happened — sitting next to her on the lawn chair and laughing so hard that we couldn't breathe, leaning over and kissing her on the mouth —

That kiss — that stupid kiss. What the hell did I do?

I never had to tell Brian about it. And now that Shannon was gone, I never had to worry that she would tell him either. But you know what? I wanted to tell my stupid, out-of-control brother. I wanted him to know that he took the best person in my life, even if I was never going to be with her. I wanted to punish Brian. He deserved to be punished.

Shannon didn't deserve any of this. Her parents didn't deserve to have their only child taken from them because of Brian. And none of us even deserved to have a person as good as Shannon in our lives.

Certainly not Joe Runnel, who just wouldn't leave her alone. Certainly not Ma, who always pretended that Brian was rambunctious and misunderstood. Certainly not me, who stood by and did nothing while Brian brought that hammer down on her head. Certainly not Brian, who just... just...couldn't control his stupid, reckless rage.

But what was I supposed to do? Brian's my brother. And since Ma was sick and couldn't protect him, I was all he had in the world.

I'll be honest. I'm not sure what's worse, being the crazy kid who committed the terrible crime, or being the one person in the world trying to protect him.

After school, I went directly to Jed's, where I'd bought the supplies last time.

I had my school backpack and I filled it with supplies for Brian. I'd brought a couple more thin blankets from home. I hadn't been able to find our sleeping bag. I bought as many cans of food as I could fit. I also got a box of plastic sporks and Chinet bowls for him to eat with. I made sure I bought a can opener, too. I almost left the store without it. That would've been great if I'd have brought him a ton of food and no way to open the cans.

Brian would probably end up on one of those websites about the stupidest people who die every year. I could just see the banner across the top of the screen: *Boy with 15 Cans of Food Starves to Death.*

Actually, it probably wouldn't say "Boy." It would probably say "Murderer."

Then I headed straight for the beach. I figured if anyone were watching, it would be harder to pick me out of the crowd of hundreds of kids walking home from school. I had on my black hoodie and the old Nats cap Brian gave me when he outgrew it. As I headed south toward the beach, I didn't see any cop cars or even any suspicious-looking regular cars. As I got farther away from school, I stopped a couple of times to tie my shoe. I glanced around and I didn't see any lone adults walking in the same direction as me.

At this point, though, I had to take the chance even if someone was watching. When I got to the beach, I walked up the block and past it. I wanted to see if anyone followed me. I didn't see anybody, so I doubled back and headed into the parking lot.

There were no cars at all. I was so paranoid that I walked all the way past the cave and down to the beach to look out at the water. I had a hunch that there might be a police boat out on the water or something.

The coast was clear—no pun intended.

Then I headed back up the trail and I found the spot easily this time. I shrugged off the backpack and put it on the ground. I got to my hands and knees and looked inside the cave. It was pitch dark. I flung the backpack forward and crawled inside.

Once I got my whole body in, I whispered, "Brian. Are you in here?"

I heard a heavy sigh. "Right here, Nate."

Suddenly the light clicked and the cave lit up. Brian sat in the corner, surrounded by food wrappers and other garbage. I stood and walked toward him. He didn't move.

He looked terrible. I guess I should've realized he might, but I hadn't been expecting it. Once my eyes adjusted to the low light, I saw that his face was pale and his eyes were bloodshot. He swatted at a nonexistent fly as I sat down in front of him.

I started unpacking the backpack. I took out the cans first and piled them neatly on the sand. I even turned the labels so they all faced the same direction. I put the can opener, the box of sporks, and the package of bowls on top of some of the cans. When I took out the blankets, I made sure the folds were still tight as I placed them neatly one on top of the other.

Then I reached to the bottom of the bag. I pulled out a long brown sock. I handled it carefully. I opened the end and slid out the bayonet. I placed it in the sand in front of the rest of the supplies. Out of all the things I brought, it was the only thing Brian seemed to notice.

"Are you okay?" I finally asked.

He didn't seem to understand the question. "What? Why wouldn't I be?"

"What's the matter with you? You look awful," I said.

"I'm not sleeping, Nate."

"Why not?"

"At first, it was because every time I heard a noise—the slam of a car door, feet sliding on the sand—I thought it was someone coming to find me. But that went away after the first night. I realized that no one knows where this place is. So I figured I would sleep last night. I was exhausted. And then, when I closed my eyes, I saw Shannon."

I nodded. "Yeah. I've been seeing her, too. That bloody smear—"

"No, no! I wasn't thinking about her like that."

Brian suddenly stood up. He stood over me. "I was thinking about when I was fourteen and I walked her to the movies that first time. We hardly said anything all the way, so I was relieved when the movie started. At least I didn't feel like I was supposed to talk then. Then there was this part in the movie when a bomb exploded suddenly, and Shannon jumped. She grabbed my hand. I locked fingers with her and we held hands for the rest of the movie and all the way home. I just kept seeing that over and over again."

He held his palms out like he wanted to continue but didn't know what to say.

"Why would that keep you awake? That's a good memory, Bri."

"I was afraid that if I fell asleep, I wouldn't be able to see it again when I woke up. I can still see every moment. I can still see Shannon pursing her lips because her mouth was dry. I can still see her standing with her arms folded, leaning against the wall when I came out of the bathroom after the movie. She gave me a shy little wave as I came back. I can still see it. Did you ever see her wave like that?" he said.

I could tell he wasn't even really talking to me. He was just speaking the thoughts in his head. Normally, I'd have let him keep going and living in

95

that beautiful memory.

But the last memory I have of Shannon when she was alive was that shy little wave. I can still see her sitting on that lawn chair after I'd kissed her — growing smaller as I walked away, trying to escape.

Except every time I see that wave and the sad smile she gave me, her eyes go blank and I see the dent form in her head. I see the blood smeared across her forehead.

"She waved at me like that the night before you killed her." I said it with as much malice as I could muster.

"What?" Brian looked down at me. His eyes searched my face. He was confused.

I stood up. "You crazy fucker! You're in here jerking off thinking about your first date while I'm out there taking care of our mother and keeping the cops from finding you! Do you even feel anything? You killed her, Brian! The girl you loved! The girl who loved you!" I tried to stop myself right there, but I couldn't. "The girl *I* loved."

As soon as I said it, I felt a warm sensation in the middle of my chest. It was like the shame was coursing through my body. But I felt relieved, too.

"What did you just say?" Brian wasn't confused anymore. I recognized the anger in his eyes.

"You heard me. I loved Shannon. I always did.

While you snuck into her house and fucked her every night, I was home in my bed thinking about her. I was thinking about how kind she was, how sweet she was, and how she really was too good for you."

"You think *you* shoulda been in her house." He'd already balled his fists.

"No. I knew she was out of my league, too. I only wish you'd have realized it and left her alone. She might still be alive, you psycho."

Brian didn't attack me immediately. He stood there, seething, but he was confused, too. I could tell he was thinking about what I was saying. I knew that somewhere deep inside of him, he knew I was right.

He stood there for a few seconds and his shoulders slumped. I thought for a second that his anger had left him, but then he lashed at me with a vicious uppercut.

It hit me on the chin and sent me reeling back. I banged hard into the wall of the cave, but I knew you couldn't dance away from Brian after a punch like that. The only thing to do was meet him head-on so I lowered my shoulder and rushed at him. I speared him in the stomach and shoved him hard to the ground.

I sprung up and sent my right hand down on

his face again and again. I knew I couldn't let up. As soon as I did, Brian would strike back.

I brought my fist up and down again, but this time, Brian tucked his head down into his chest and I hit the top of his head. It was like punching a rock. I felt the jolt in my hand all the way up my wrist. Before I knew it, Brian had sent a fist up from between my hands that bloodied my nose.

I tried to grab his arms to keep him from hitting me again, but he was too strong. He shoved my arm off and hit me on the side of the face with a haymaker that knocked me clear off of him.

I rolled in the sand and tried to get up. He was on top of me in a second. He used his weight like Marisconi. He leaned all the weight of his body onto my chest and grabbed my hair so I couldn't even move my head out of the way of his fist. He'd hit me with one, two, three rapid punches when my hand, flailing in the sand, hit something metal. I groped until I felt my hand close around the bayonet and I swung it up and brought it as hard as I could into Brian's shoulder.

He fell off of me this time. I scrambled to my feet and held the blade out at him. He was standing, stunned, holding his shoulder. There was blood darkening his shirt all the way down the sleeve.

"What the fuck, Nate! Are you gonna kill me?"

"I'd like to." I meant it.

"Do you hate me that much?"

"No, but you deserve it." I spat after I said it. I could taste the salty blood in my mouth.

"You're right. I do."

And just like I'd seen a hundred times before, all of Brian's anger was gone. He was suddenly small, frail, and lost. His shoulders hunched. He breathed deeply and dropped his head.

"You're right, Nate. Go ahead and do it." He dropped to his knees in front of me. "I deserve it. If you wanna stab me first and make me feel it before you cut my throat, that's fine. I deserve it all. I don't even know what kind of punishment is fit for what I've done, for what I am. But you're right, Nate. Whatever it is, I deserve it."

For one insane moment, my body tensed up and I felt like I was a second away from bringing this blade down in my brother's neck.

"I killed Shannon. I've made Ma suffer my whole life. And you. You're the only person I have left and I almost killed you. I don't even know what I am, Nate. Sick? Crazy? I don't even know if there's a word for what I am."

I threw the bayonet down into the sand. "You're the fucking hydra, Brian."

"What the hell is that?" he said.

99

"It was this monster with nine heads in the old Greek myths. Hercules had to kill it. Except every time he cut off one of its heads, two more sprouted from its neck. That's you!" I pointed at him. "Every time you have a problem, me and Ma kill ourselves to fix it. Then the next time you get mad there's twice as much shit to deal with. And you're getting worse! This isn't a game, Bri. You're not a kid fighting at school or telling the cops to go fuck themselves! You really did it this time! You killed her!"

Brian's shoulders sagged. He looked down. He suddenly looked very small. It was like he was trying to shrink back into himself so I couldn't hurt him. But I wanted to hurt him.

I drew the words out slowly, so that every one hit him like a punch. "You killed Shannon because Joe Runnel came to her house."

He tried to look up at me. "That's not—"

"Yeah, it is, Bri. You took one problem and you—" I spread my arms out wide. "You made all of this."

Brian looked down again. "Maybe I am a monster, Nate. Maybe it's as simple as that."

CHAPTER EIGHT

I had to work that night. When I got to Maltby's, I rang the bell in the back and I expected Dylan or one of the other kids to open the door. Mr. Harris opened it this time. Mr. Harris was normally a friendly and kind old man, but when he opened the door, I could immediately tell something was wrong. His face was more wrinkled than any other person's that I'd ever seen. I always thought it was because he smiled so much. Tonight, however, he looked at me with pity as I passed him and walked into the back of the store. Then I saw Detective Marisconi and I understood.

"Hello, Nathan. Would you come with me to the counter?" Marisconi asked. He was pretending to be polite, but I could hear the happiness in his voice when he spoke.

I looked at Mr. Harris and he shook his head

gravely at me. Marisconi and I walked through the rest of the back room. I could feel Marisconi's eyes on me. My face was still swollen from the fight with Brian. Ma hadn't even noticed it, but Marisconi did.

"What happened to your face?" he asked as we came out the door to the front of the store. I shook my head and didn't say anything.

Suddenly, Marisconi nudged me with his elbow.

"Look up there, tough guy," he said, pointing to the decorative birdcage with the big fake parrot in it. "Do you notice anything?"

I stared at the bird for a few moments. Then I saw it. In the bird's mouth was a small lens. A hidden camera.

I looked quickly back at Marisconi, who was looking over at me and grinning from ear to ear.

"Mr. Harris just showed me some security footage of you stealing money out of the register yesterday. He called me to look at it and he just asked me if I thought he should press charges."

I was in trouble. Mr. Harris never mentioned anything about a security camera in the store. That was probably by design, though. That old bastard wasn't checking the tapes to see if any customers stole anything, he was checking it to see if any of the employees were stealing. I guess I fell right into that one.

I didn't say anything. I just stared at Marisconi as blankly as I could.

"Mr. Harris estimated that you stole somewhere between twenty and thirty dollars. From what I saw, that sounds about right. Normally, I wouldn't recommend pressing charges against somebody for so little, but you're sort of a special case, aren't you, Nathan?"

I continued to stare at him.

"Do you have the money on you, Nathan? Would you like to return it?"

I didn't move for a few seconds, and then I shook my head. I could feel my eyes sting as tears tried to find their way out of them.

"That's what I thought, Sport-o." Marisconi turned to the back room. "Mr. Harris," he called.

When Mr. Harris got to the front, Marisconi spoke to him very properly. It was like he was a banker telling a client how to invest his money.

"Mr. Harris, I'm going to recommend that you press charges against Mr. Keller, here. He's stolen cash from you, and you have the right to get your money back."

I finally spoke up. "For thirty bucks? You're really telling him to press charges against me for thirty bucks? Isn't that a big waste of everyone's time?"

"Oh, no, Nathan. I don't believe it's a waste at all." Marisconi couldn't hold back the smirk that was creeping onto his face.

That's when I realized what was happening. They weren't really going to charge me with stealing the money. Marisconi was going to use this to try and get me to tell him where Brian was.

Mr. Harris didn't say anything else. The old man just turned and went into the back room.

Then, Marisconi made a big show of cuffing me right there behind the counter and he led me out toward his car, which was parked out front. I had to walk past a couple of customers in the store eating waffle cones as well as a few people on the street. I didn't recognize any of them, but they were certainly very interested in seeing a cop arrest some punk teenager.

Marisconi put me in the back of the car and shut the door. Then, he stood outside the car door and made a call on his cell phone. He spoke for only a few seconds. What the hell was he up to?

We rode in silence to the station. The station was a rundown, one-story building in the oldest part of town, the south edge near the beach. When we came in, Marisconi took me into the lobby and we went up to the reception area, where a police officer was seated in a glass cubicle.

The cop in the reception cubicle processed me. I tried to say as little as possible. I only made brief responses to all of the questions, which were mostly about my name, address, and the like. Remember, I didn't even have a driver's license yet.

When we were done, Marisconi picked up my file and carried it into the main office, where the cops had their desks. He walked me over to the largest one in the corner of the room, stood next to the chair, and pushed me into the seat. He undid one of my cuffs and then cuffed me to the chair and I sat down. He was really putting it on now.

There were no other cops or criminals in this area with us. We were alone.

"Nathan, let's be honest. I didn't come here to talk about the money you stole. We're not gonna charge you for that. We need to talk about Brian."

"There's nothing to talk about, Detective." I bit off the last word so that he would get the idea that I thought he was a joke. "I don't know where he is. I haven't seen him since before Shannon died," I said.

"Nathan, I don't believe that's true. I think you know where he is." Marisconi leaned back in his chair and put his hands behind his head. "And you're not going anywhere until you tell me."

"Fuck you."

"Watch it, schoolboy. Your mama's not here to save you this time. Nathan, I'm gonna give you one chance to do the right thing here, before I start to put on the pressure. What is the matter with you? Don't you realize that your brother is a sick kid? He ended someone's life."

It wasn't *someone*. It was Shannon.

I suddenly tried to find something interesting in the tile pattern on the floor.

"Nathan, you're a good kid. I've never had to deal with you the way I had to deal with Brian. You can control yourself. You work hard in school. You've taken care of your mother ever since Dan Howe left her. And now she's sick. All this stuff with you and your brother is gonna kill her if you keep dragging it out." Mariscioni stopped. He sat there staring at me, letting that sink in.

I felt the same hot shame fill my chest that I'd felt in the cave, but I didn't move. I didn't make a sound.

Mariscioni finally cleared his throat. I still refused to look at him. He stood up and walked around the desk to stand directly over me.

"Nathan, if you don't tell me where Brian is, I'm going to put you up as an accessory to murder," he said.

I finally looked up at him.

"That seems like a pretty big jump—from you stole thirty bucks to you helped a murderer," I said. I wanted Marisconi to think I wasn't afraid of him, even though I was.

He stared at me for a few moments. He wasn't used to punk kids not doing what he wanted. He was intimidating enough that most people gave him what he wanted when he asked for it. But I wasn't falling for it this time.

"I'd like to make my phone call," I said like I knew what I was doing. Hell, I'd watched *Law & Order*.

Marisconi picked up the phone from the other end of the desk and placed it in front of me.

"Go ahead, Sport-o."

I dialed our home number and waited for Ma to pick up. I knew it might take her awhile to get to the phone, so I didn't get nervous when she didn't pick up after a couple of rings. On the eighth ring, she finally picked up.

"Hello," she croaked. I could tell she had been sleeping and the phone had woken her up.

"Ma, it's me. Marisconi picked me up for stealing money at work and he's trying to get me to tell him where Brian is," I said.

"Did you tell him?" She was fully awake

now.

"No. I don't know where he is," I said. "Can you get them to release me?"

"Put Frank on the phone," Ma said.

I held the phone out to him. "She wants to talk to you."

He took the receiver and leaned back in his chair again. I could hear Ma talking quickly and angrily on the phone, but I couldn't hear what she was saying.

"No, Ellen. He's a minor. I'm not releasing him to anyone except a parent or guardian. No, there's no bail, but you'll have to come down and get him if you want him," he said.

So that was his plan all along. Marisconi knew Ma wasn't well enough to come and get me out, so I'd have to sit here with him until I told him what he wanted to know. He really was a scumbag to use Ma's cancer against us.

I could hear what sounded like a sob from the other end of the phone as Ma continued to talk. Suddenly, she stopped. She then spoke a few short sentences. Her voice softened and the last thing she said sounded like a question.

Marisconi's eyebrows nearly met as his eyes glazed over with confusion.

"A blue one. With pinstripes. There's a

design like a half moon on the tie." I realized just then that Ma was asking what he was wearing. What was she doing? Had the chemo finally killed the cells in her mind, too?

Ma said something else and Marisconi answered. "Okay, Ellen. Fine." Then he hung up the phone. He looked confused and slightly amused.

"What did she say?" I asked.

"The normal stuff at first—about how I couldn't hold you and that I had to release you. But then she started asking me what I was wearing. I don't know what the hell that was all about. Does that mean anything to you?"

I shook my head. I really didn't know what it meant.

Just then, the cop who processed me came into the office.

"Frank. They're here," he said.

Marisconi stood up. "All right. Give me one second." He reached down and took the cuff off my wrist. He pulled me up by the arm and led me to an office.

He opened the door. There was a large wooden table with five chairs scattered around it. "Sit down and don't move. I'll be right back." As soon as I went inside, he closed the door. I heard the lock click. I stared at the door for a few seconds and then I walked around to the chair farthest from the door. I sat down and waited. What was Marisconi up to?

I heard Marisconi talking in a low, urgent voice as he approached the door. He opened it and led in two people — Shannon's parents.

Bill Carter came in first, and his round, red face looked smeared by the tears that he was wiping off of his cheeks. He was wearing a gray T-shirt and I could see the pack of cigarettes poking out of the pocket. Susan Carter walked in slowly, dressed in a white zippered sweatshirt, and her eyes immediately locked with mine. There were no tears in her eyes. I could feel the fire in her stare. She was angry.

"Mr. and Mrs. Carter, please sit down." Marisconi pointed at two of the chairs across from me.

Marisconi sat down between us. He looked at me and nodded very slowly. "All right, Nathan. I believe you know Shannon's parents. They're here tonight because I need to convince you to do the right thing, and up to this point, you've refused. You have a choice. You can finally tell me where Brian is or you can look Shannon's parents in their faces and tell them that their daughter's life was worth nothing. You can tell them that they don't deserve justice for the death of their little girl. It's up to you."

I dropped my gaze to the table. What could I do?

"Mr. Carter, would you like to say something to Nathan?" Marisconi said gently.

"Nathan, I know you're trying to protect your brother. I get that. But he took our baby. We came home from a nice night at the resort and we found our house in shambles. All of our stuff was broken and some things were missing. I thought we'd been robbed. But my first thought wasn't about any of that shit. I just wanted to find Shannon and make sure she was okay. We ran up to her room and she wasn't there. Then I remembered that she likes to watch TV in the basement, so I went down there. Her ma stayed up in her room and called her cell phone. When I reached the bottom of the stairs, I heard the phone ringing. Then I saw the coffee table knocked over and on the floor…"

He suddenly rubbed the bridge of his nose. It was like he was trying to rub it hard enough so that the tears wouldn't interrupt him.

"Then I saw my baby lyin' there. Her skull was cracked open and there was blood all down the side of her face. I couldn't do a damn thing. I stood there and stared at her for what seemed like forever. It's like it wasn't real."

He suddenly snapped his mouth shut again and this time there was no way to stop the tears. He sobbed uncontrollably. His whole body shook and it was like he couldn't breathe. I watched him for a few seconds and then I put my arms on the table in front of me and buried my head in them.

"Don't you dare look away, you son of a bitch!" Shannon's mother stood up and reached across the table. She grabbed one of my hands roughly and pulled it up. "Look at him, you coward!" she screamed. I jumped back and stared at her.

Marisconi stood up and waved her arm away from me. "Mrs. Carter, please."

"Sue, sit down." Bill Carter reached out and gently tried to push his wife back into her seat.

Mrs. Carter shrugged her husband's hand off of her. "Tell us where he is!" She slammed her palm on the table. "He killed her and then he tried to cover it up—that fucking coward! He wrecked the house and left her there. He tried to make everyone think it was a robbery! What kind of a sick bastard does that?" She was leaning hard across the table. I had no doubt that if Marisconi wasn't here, she would've attacked me.

"How do you know it wasn't a robbery?" It had been my idea, so I figured I'd better try and sell it to them. We left the house a mess trying to make it look like a robbery. It was the only way I could think of to shift suspicion away from Brian. I knew it wouldn't really work, but I didn't know what else to do.

Marisconi answered my question. "Joe Runnel...and this." Marisconi reached into his pocket and took out a cell phone. It was Brian's. I forgot he left it at Shannon's house. Marisconi put it on the table in front of me.

Marisconi explained that he knew about the party the night before. The police had gotten a few calls from the neighbors about the music being too loud and kids wandering up and down the block being obnoxious. He tracked down a few of the kids who'd been there, and all any of them could talk about was how Brian had beaten the shit out of Joe Runnel.

"When I tracked down Runnel, he told me all about the fight the night before, but he also told me about how he went to Shannon's in the morning and that Brian came screeching down the street and that he just ran. So it's pretty certain that the last person to see her alive was Brian. We searched the basement and found the phone. Then we found the hammer and it had Brian's fingerprints all over it."

I was waiting for Marisconi to tell me that Joe

Runnel had told him I was there, too. But he didn't. Apparently, Runnel didn't tell Marisconi about me for some reason. Or if he did, Marisconi wasn't saying anything. I hardly know Joe Runnel at all so I don't know why he would intentionally leave me out of it. Of course, there was the possibility that Joe Runnel was so scared when he saw Brian that morning, that he didn't even notice me. I figured if Marisconi knew I was there, he would play that card now to really put the pressure on me. He'd have me for a lot more than stealing money out of the cash register at Maltby's.

Marisconi sighed. "You've got to tell me where he is now, Nathan. Shannon's parents deserve that much."

I looked up at Shannon's parents. They were the most pathetic people I'd ever seen — and I don't mean that in an insulting way. I'd never felt worse for any two people in my entire life. Shannon's father was looking at me expectantly, like he was hoping with everything he had that I was finally going to tell. Shannon's mother seemed to have worn herself out. She'd sat back in her chair and was covering her face with her hand.

"I don't know where — "

"Stop with that bullshit, Nathan!" Marisconi screamed this time. He got up and grabbed me by the collar of my shirt. He pulled me to my feet. He held me there and stared into my face. I think he would've stood there forever and waited until I finally cracked.

But there was a knock at the door.

Marisconi let go of my shirt and stalked away from me. He opened the door and it was the cubicle cop again. He whispered something in Marisconi's ear. Suddenly, Marisconi looked up at me. I heard him say to the cop, "He's not his legal guardian."

The cop whispered back into Marisconi's ear.

Marisconi put his head down. He looked up at me again and pushed the door wide open.

"You're free to go, Nathan."

Mr. Carter stood up this time. "What?" Mrs. Carter didn't. It was like she'd given up already.

"I have no choice, Mr. Carter. A legal guardian has come to pick him up. I can't hold him." Marisconi dropped his eyes. I bet he promised the Carters that this would work and he was humiliated now that it hadn't.

But what I didn't understand was how Ma even got down here. She couldn't drive. Hell, I wasn't even sure she could get out of bed by herself anymore.

"Go on, Nathan. Get out of here. This officer will provide you with your instructions and give

115

you back your personal belongings."

I walked back to the cubicle and waited while the officer went back inside and started to process my release. The cop was talking, but I wasn't really paying attention. I was staring through the glass and into the lobby on the other side. At first, I didn't recognize the broad-shouldered man standing there. I'd seen the man's blue eyes somewhere before, but his chiseled face was unfamiliar to me. Then it hit me. I'd never seen him without a beard before.

It was Dan Howe.

CHAPTER NINE

I stood there for several minutes, looking through the glass at Dan Howe. He wasn't quite the same man I remembered. Not only was the beard gone, but he also looked sharper than I remembered him. He'd been a beer-drinking biker when he was married to Ma, but he wasn't quite as heavy now. His chest was broad and it stuck out, instead of his belly. His dark brown hair, which was peppered with gray, was very neat. He was wearing a T-shirt and jeans, but he was also wearing a sport coat over the shirt.

Right as the cubicle cop buzzed the door open, Marisconi came out of the office. He elbowed me out of the way and went through the door. I followed quickly on his heels.

"I'd like a word with you, Mr. Howe," Marisconi said. "I want to know how you're involved in all of this. You haven't been married to Ellen in what, three or four years? Suddenly you're here to pick up Nathan."

Dan looked Marisconi up and down. "Ellen called me. Said she was desperate. She said you were holding Nathan and that she was too sick to come and bail him out. She told me you knew that she was too sick to come and get him and that you were just trying to make him suffer."

"How did you know you were still listed as a legal guardian of Nathan's?" Marisconi shot back.

"I didn't. Ellen told me. I don't know what any of this is about. All I know is what Ellen told me. I'm just here to pick up the kid." He looked at me. "C'mon, Nate."

I started past Marisconi but he grabbed me by the shoulder. He screamed at Dan. "His brother killed somebody and ran away to hide. This kid knows where he is and he won't tell me!"

Dan looked startled for a moment, but then gained control of himself. He sighed. "Okay, Frank. I don't doubt it. I'm just trying to help Ellen out, all right?"

Marisconi took his hand off my shoulder and pointed at Dan. "You tell her that I'm gonna get that little son of a bitch and I'm gonna nail his ass to the wall!" I looked at the finger Marisconi was pointing. It was shaking. Marisconi had been involved in a lot of our shit over the years, but I'd never seen him this close to losing control. It was like watching Brian.

Dan nodded. "Oh, by the way, Frank, Ellen wanted me to give you a message, too."

"Yeah?"

"Yeah. She wanted me to tell you that you're a slob. She said that every suit you own looks like you pulled it out of your ass. Her words. Not mine." Dan put his hand on my shoulder and walked me out of the police station.

I had to bite my lip to keep from howling in front of Marisconi.

When we finally got to the car, I got in and burst out laughing. Dan looked over at me and even cracked a smile. "I was telling the truth. Your ma told me to tell him that."

"I know. I know. She says that about Marisconi all the time," I said when I could catch my breath again.

It wasn't until we were on the road that I finally realized we were in a really nice car. It was brand new. It still had the new car smell.

"What kind of car is this?" I asked.

"It's a Mercedes, S-Class."

"Wow." I looked around the car in awe.

I'd never been in a Mercedes before. I remember when he was married to Ma that Dan drove an old Ford F-150 pickup truck. He used it to drag around groundskeeping equipment and sod most of the time.

"What happened to your truck?" I said.

"I got rid of it. I don't do groundskeeping anymore. I'm the regional coordinator of buildings and grounds for the entire company. I mostly work with architects and designers on renovation and addition projects for all the resorts that the Champagne Company owns in this region. From here all the way to Florida."

Wow. Dan had really moved up in the world since he got rid of us.

I sat there wondering what life would've been like if Dan had stayed married to my mother. I wondered if maybe Ma would be getting better treatment for her cancer because he had a good job and probably really good insurance. I also wondered if maybe Brian wouldn't be in trouble either. Maybe Dan could've gotten him some help before he did anything crazy like this. I doubted it, though.

In fact, I'll bet the only reason Dan was able to get ahead was because he didn't let himself get dragged down by all of us. Maybe it's what Shannon should've done. If Shannon had ditched us, right now she'd be studying for her SATs instead of lying in the morgue at the Duffle County Hospital.

I know Dan left my mother. I know he loved her, but he just didn't want to deal with Brian all the time—going to the police station or the school and fighting with cops, social workers, and administrators to get him out of trouble, fighting with Ma about getting him some sort of treatment or medication. I know that's why he left. I know Ma was never the same after that either. But I just couldn't be mad at the guy. Brian made everyone's life hard. How could I blame Dan for not letting Brian ruin his life, too?

In fact, I was a little jealous. There were times I wondered what life would be like if Brian didn't exist. I wondered what it would be like to be a normal family. The truth is, I'll never know.

We drove in silence for a few minutes until Dan finally asked, "Do you want to tell me about this thing with your brother?"

At first, I tried to give him the short version, like I used to when he'd ask about a book I was reading. But when I got to the part where Brian killed Shannon, it all just started to pour out of me. I told him about how Brian went crazy and hit her with the hammer. I told him how we trashed her house to make it look like a robbery. I told him that Brian was hiding, but I didn't tell him where.

I even started to tell him about school and meeting Celia. I'm not even sure what he was hearing, but once I'd started I couldn't stop. I told him about stealing the money to buy stuff for Brian and being arrested and Shannon's parents and everything.

When I was done, I leaned back in the seat, trying to catch my breath. I was exhausted. I didn't even realize that we'd stopped and were sitting in the parking lot of JC's, the diner off the highway at the edge of town.

Neither of us said anything for a long time. We just sat in the car and stared at the brightly lit sign set against the night sky. I didn't even know what time it was.

I left out the part about being in love with Shannon. I didn't tell him about the kiss either. I didn't want to explain any of that to him. In fact, I didn't want to explain any of that to anyone ever. It hurt too much.

"I figured you might want something to eat," Dan finally said.

We went into the diner. At first, I thought maybe I would just get some soup or something, but once I sat down, I realized how hungry I was. I ate soup, a burger, fries, and Dan ordered me a hot dog after that. I finished that, too.

We didn't talk much while we ate. Dan just ate a turkey sandwich. He explained that his cholesterol was high and he was trying to eat right. He was so different than the man who used to grill up an entire box of hamburgers for the four of us. We always finished them, but usually only because Brian and Dan ate three or four apiece.

When we did talk, Dan tried to make normal conversation. He asked me about school and what I was reading. It was actually the most normal I'd felt in a long time. When we were done, he drove me home and before I got out of the car, he gave me his cell phone number, just in case I ever needed it.

I doubted that I would ever call him again, but I appreciated him giving me the number. I never knew my dad, and I know that Dan was never much of a replacement for him anyway, but it was as close as I was going to get.

When I was about to get out of the car, he reached over and extended his hand. I shook it. His big hand was still rough. Even though he was an executive now, he'd never be rid of the bumps and calluses from all the hard years of digging and mowing. Those marks would never go away. I knew what that was like.

When I came into the house, Ma was asleep on the couch again. I'm not even sure how she got there. I was always worried about her moving around the house when I wasn't home. I tried to wake her, but she was really groggy. I finally picked her up and carried her into the bedroom.

As I pulled the covers up over her, she came to a little. She reached up and touched my face. Her bony hand was ice cold.

"Are you okay?"

"Yeah, Ma. I'm fine. Dan picked me up a couple of hours ago. He took me to eat. We talked for a while. Did you eat?"

"I'm not hungry, sweetheart." She patted my hair gently. Even though it was dimly lit, I could tell that Ma's eyes were glassy and unfocused.

"Are you in a lot of pain?"

She ignored my question. "Did Dan give Marisconi my message?"

I snorted and nodded.

"Good. At least that son of a bitch is good for something."

"How did you even think to call Dan, Ma?"

"When Dan and I first got married, we were convinced that we were going to be together forever. I thought he was going to be a real father—" All of a sudden, she started coughing. I had to pull her body up off the bed and lean her forward because it seemed like she was choking when she was on her back. When she could finally take her regular, shallow breaths again, I laid her back on the pillows.

"That's okay, Ma. You can tell me —"

"No, no." She was intent on telling me. "I made Dan file for legal guardianship so that you boys could be put on the good insurance he got through the resort. I never changed it even..." she trailed off. I thought she'd fallen asleep in mid-sentence.

"Ma," I whispered.

She continued like nothing had happened. "When Marisconi played that bullshit that he wasn't going to release you to anyone but a legal guardian, I figured I had no choice but to call Dan. Thank God he was in town."

I kissed her forehead. "It's too bad we don't have Dan's good insurance now, huh?"

"We'll manage."

I sighed. "Well, it was a good idea. Thanks, Ma. Good night."

****

The next morning, Ma was still sleeping when I left for school. As I wandered the halls that morning, I found myself looking for Celia. Now that I thought about it, I didn't remember ever seeing her in the halls before, but maybe I just hadn't noticed.

125

I was anxious as fourth period ended because I wanted to rush down to the library and see if Celia was there. I decided not to run there or anything, but I wanted to see her.

When I entered the library, I went straight to the row of cubicles in the back corner, but she wasn't there. I could feel the air leave my chest. I was disappointed. It was just then that I heard a voice behind me.

"You came back, huh?"

It was Celia. She was standing with her backpack slung over her shoulder and she was leaning on one foot. She had a smirk on her face as she looked up at me.

Now that we were both standing, I realized how much taller I was than her. She barely came up to my shoulder. I could feel myself smiling at her, but I realized after a few seconds I hadn't said anything yet. I panicked and said the first thing I could think of.

"Um, yeah." Sometimes I'm so damn smooth I want to punch myself in the face.

She walked past me and sat in the last cubicle like she had yesterday. She started taking out books and notebooks and piling them on the desk. She wasn't looking at me, but she still had the smirk on her face.

I pulled out the chair next to her and sat down. I faced her.

"Listen. I want to apologize about yesterday. I wasn't very nice to you."

She looked up from her books. "It's okay. I was being kinda rude. All you wanted was to be left alone and I just butted right into your life. You seem better today, though. Is the problem with your brother getting any better?"

"Actually, no. The cops arrested me last night. They tried to make me tell them where he's hiding."

A little wrinkle appeared on her forehead as she looked at me. I liked that look. "Really?"

"Really."

She stopped pretending to organize her books. "Are you okay?"

"Actually, yeah. I am." I was being honest. I really didn't know how I was supposed to feel right then. All I know is that I was excited to be next to Celia. I was excited that she was talking to me. I was excited that she was looking at me like she cared if I was okay. I just wanted to keep talking to her.

Then she hit me with a question I didn't expect. "What's your name anyway?"

I realized then that she'd introduced herself to me yesterday and that she'd probably heard I

127

was the kid with the psycho-killer for a brother, but I hadn't told her my name.

"Nathan. Nathan Keller." I extended my hand.

She looked at my hand. She shook her head playfully and shook it. "Hi, Nathan." She was probably thinking about how she'd extended her hand to me yesterday and I didn't take it.

We talked for the rest of the lunch period. Celia told me all about her family and how they moved here from Michigan so that her dad could work at one of the resort docks. He was a boat mechanic. He'd worked for a manufacturer before they moved the factory out of the country, and now he made his living servicing rich people's boats. She told me her family moved here last year, but she didn't really know anybody. She didn't socialize much here at school and she spent most of the time after school taking care of her little sister while her parents worked all sorts of crazy hours.

I told her a little bit about myself, too. I told her about Ma having cancer and not being able to do much. I tried to make it sound manageable, though. I was pretty sure the cancer was going to kill Ma, and probably soon, but somehow I didn't want to say that in front of Celia. I didn't want to upset her. It didn't make any sense, though. Why would she be upset?

When the bell rang, we both started to pack up and head out in separate directions, but I wanted to see her again right away.

I looked down at the floor and said it quickly, "So do you think maybe I could walk you home after school?"

After I asked the question, I took a chance and glanced up at her. There was no mistake about it. She didn't smirk this time. She smiled. I could actually see her teeth.

"Sure…Nathan."

"Great. How about if I meet you by the trophy case next to the office?"

She swung the backpack across her shoulders and held the straps with her hands.

"Okay." She bit her lip. I could tell she wanted to say something. This time she looked down at the floor. "I have study hall next period…you know, if you wanna text me or something," she said.

"My teacher probably won't like it, but sure."

She laughed. We exchanged phone numbers.

She started away and I just stood there staring at her. She made a quick turn and took a few backward steps. She raised her hand and gave me a shy, little wave. She turned around and before I knew it, she was gone.

129

I finally started moving and realized that I was going to be late for sixth period. Mrs. Shelver was usually really tough on students who were tardy. She had a big poster board at the front of her room that had every student's absences and tardies on it. I had a couple of tardies already, even though it was only the beginning of the school year. I didn't need to cause myself any more trouble. I ran.

I was hoping that maybe she would've heard about Brian and given me a break, but as I came up to her door, there was one of the new deans, whose name I didn't even know, standing with Mrs. Shelver.

She nodded in my direction. "That's him, John." Mrs. Shelver turned and went into her classroom.

"Nathan?" the new dean asked. He was a young guy with really curly blonde hair. He didn't look angry. He looked sad.

I nodded.

"We just got the call. They took your mother to the hospital this morning in an ambulance. Why don't you come down to the office and—"

I didn't hear the rest. I bolted down the hall toward the staircase. I had to get to the hospital. I had to get to Ma.

"Nathan! Nathan!" the dean yelled after me.

Twenty-seven minutes and one bumpy bus ride

later, I walked into the Intensive Care Unit at Duffle County Hospital. When I got to the desk, there was a lanky doctor with sandy hair sitting there looking intently at a computer screen.

"I'm looking for my mother, Ellen Howe," I said.

The doctor put his finger up as if to signal for me to wait. Without thinking, I grabbed it.

"I'm not waiting. Where's my mother?"

The doctor pulled his hand away from me and got out of his chair. He stared at me like he was afraid. I suppose he expected me to wait patiently.

Right then a nurse in a blue smock came up. "Can I help you?" she said.

"I'm looking for my mother, Ellen Howe."

The nurse checked the chart in front of her. "She's in 416. This way."

As I followed the nurse, I gave the doctor one more hard look.

When we got to Ma's room, it was dark and smelled like rubbing alcohol. I hate the smell of hospitals. When I approached her bed, I saw that they'd attached an oxygen tube to her nose and there was saline attached to her IV.

"She's very weak. She's dehydrated and her T-cell count is extremely low."

"I know. She's undergoing a second round of

131

chemo and it's hurting her a lot. She hasn't been eating or drinking much. But I don't understand, how did she get here?"

"Apparently, your mother tried to get up this morning and felt dizzy and weak. She stumbled over to the phone and was able to call 911. She told the operator her address and that she was sick. That was it."

"What do you mean?" I asked.

The nurse shrugged her shoulders. "The operator kept trying to talk to her, but they think she passed out then. She's lucky she was able to do that much. The paramedics got there and found her unconscious on the floor," she said.

"Jesus."

The nurse reached out and touched my shoulder. "I'm sorry."

According to the nurse, there wasn't anything new about Ma's symptoms. They were just much worse because her immune system was so weak. She would have to stay in the ICU. She was running a fever and they weren't sure if she had water in her lungs or if there was an infection somewhere.

I suddenly felt like a little kid. I looked over at Ma. I had a million questions I wanted to ask, but I couldn't find the words. I started to ask a question, but I just stuttered, "So this infection, if she has one,

I mean..." I couldn't go on.

The nurse kept her eyes on me. "What about the infection?"

I looked back at the nurse. It was easier to talk if I wasn't watching Ma struggle to breathe. "Is this why she's been sick the whole time during this round of chemo?"

The nurse shrugged again, but her green eyes softened. "Maybe. We don't know."

The nurse didn't tell me this, but I'd been there with Ma when the cancer doctor had told us how important it was for her to keep clean and ward off infections. A serious enough infection could kill her — and she may have had one for weeks. I had a bad feeling about all this.

I stayed with Ma the rest of the day. Visiting hours ended at nine, but the nurse asked me if I wanted to stay longer. She told me she could bring in a chair from the waiting room to sleep in. It was nice of her.

The whole time I was there, we never got a visit from the doctor. I had a feeling that maybe the lanky doctor with the finger was her doctor and he wasn't in any hurry to come and talk to me.

I decided it might be better if I got out of there. This way the doctor could come and do whatever he needed for Ma without worrying about me. Plus,

Brian needed to know about this.

As I left the hospital, I headed back toward our neighborhood and the beach.

It took me around an hour to walk to the east end of town. By then, it was very dark because it was cloudy. Every time I'd passed an area without a streetlight near it, I felt like I was walking with my eyes closed. In one of these expanses of dark, I tried waving my hand in front of my face. I couldn't see it.

That's when I finally remembered.

"Celia," I said out loud.

I'd forgotten that I was supposed to meet her after school by the trophy case. I took out my phone and flipped to her name in my contacts. I didn't hit the button, though. What would I say to explain all of this?

I didn't think I could feel worse than I did when I left the hospital, beginning the long trek to tell Brian that our mother was dying, but I did. I was thinking about the desperate apology I'd have to make to get her to even talk to me again when I was struck by something. Celia would understand. She would forgive me.

I didn't know why I thought that, but I did. I only met Celia yesterday and she certainly had no reason to give me another chance after I'd been so rude to her yesterday and then I stood her up today. But I thought about her…and that moment when she came across the back of the library to talk to me…when she told me the most painful and difficult thing that's probably ever happened in her life… She was so much different than any other person I'd ever met. She was so much more — I don't know what to say to describe her — human, maybe?

If there was anyone in the world who would understand, it was Celia. I was sure of it.

I put the phone back in my pocket.

Near the beach there were plenty of streetlights, and an orange glow radiated from many of the houses I passed.

When I got to the parking lot, there was an old Crown Victoria sitting in the center by itself. I couldn't see the person inside, but he or she had the window open and I could see the smoke rising as the person exhaled.

I went up the path quickly. I was glad when one of the turns put the car in the parking lot out of sight.

It was so dark I had to use the light from my phone to find the entrance to the cave. Once I did, I knelt down. I could see the light coming from inside. At least Brian wasn't sitting in the dark like he'd been the last time I came.

He was dozing in middle of the cave when I crawled in. He was wrapped tightly in the blankets I'd brought him and he was snoring loudly. I crawled over and nudged him. He wouldn't wake. I grabbed his shoulders with both hands and shook him roughly.

Suddenly his eyes popped open and he brought the bayonet up into my face. He must've been sleeping with it on him, just in case anyone came and found him in the night.

"Oh, Nate. It's you. Did you bring me some more food? All I've got left is — "

"No. I didn't bring anything tonight. I'll bring you something tomorrow. Listen, Bri. Ma's sick."

Brian pushed himself up on his elbows. "What do you mean? What's wrong?"

I told Brian all about Ma's condition. When I was done, he shook his head.

"What did she look like in the hospital?" he asked.

I didn't answer right away. "Not good. She looked like..." I didn't know how to finish the sentence. I didn't have to.

Brian fell back on the sand. He put his hands over his eyes and began to cry. These weren't silent tears escaping his eyes while he tried to keep a stoic face. He was crying hard — and loud. He was crying the way a little kid does when he can't find his mother.

I put my head down on the cool sand. After a few seconds, I was crying too. I wasn't as loud as Brian, but I couldn't control the tears, my short breaths, or the sobs that kept convulsing my body.

I still had my head down when Brian said it. "I've got to see her."

If there was one thing in the world that could've stopped me from crying, that was it. "What? Are you nuts?"

"I'm gonna get caught anyway, Nate. I can't live in here forever. Marisconi isn't gonna stop until he gets me." Brian was right. I didn't say that to him, but I knew that Marisconi would never give up looking for him.

"You could leave, Bri. We could get you out of here," I said.

"Maybe, Nate. But first I gotta see Ma."

And I knew that was the way it would have to be. To be honest, I'd have probably said the same thing in Brian's shoes. We both knew that this could be it. Ma could die and I understood that. But I also understood that Brian needed to see her. She'd tried so hard to protect him his whole life, and they left off so badly with each other that Brian wouldn't be able to live with himself if she died before he could see her again. He didn't tell me, but I think what Brian wanted most was a chance to apologize.

I know Brian had done some terrible things. But deep down, I know that there are times when he realizes the trouble he's caused and that it nearly crushes him. No wonder he's crazy.

"You can't stop me, Nate. Tomorrow morning, I'm going to see Ma in the hospital."

"Yeah. Okay." I tried to think about how we could get Brian in and out of there without getting caught.

Then it hit me. I took out my phone and flipped through the contacts. I stopped on Dan Howe's phone number.

He did tell me to call if I needed anything.

CHAPTER TEN

It was late afternoon the next day. I was in the passenger's seat of Dan Howe's Mercedes as we sped down Ocean Boulevard to the west end of town. Brian was lying on the floor in the back.

"You two are completely crazy," Dan said, checking the rearview mirror. I'm sure he was looking out to see if any cops were following us.

I slouched in the seat. I was wearing my black hoodie and Brian's old Nats hat. I had the hood up and my sunglasses on. I was wearing a pair of faded jeans and white gym shoes. I'd tried to pick out clothes that no one would notice. Today, I didn't want anyone to notice me.

I looked back at Brian behind the seat. His jeans were faded, too. They were only a little lighter than mine. No one would notice that. His shoes were a little cleaner than mine, though. I licked my thumb and tried to rub off one of the dark scuffs on my shoe.

This was never gonna work and I knew it. I think Brian knew it, too. Knowing you're gonna lose, but fighting to the end anyway—I used to think that was the definition of courage, but now I know that it's really the definition of desperation.

"Don't worry, Dan. No one's gonna notice," I said. "We'll be in and out of there before you know it."

When we pulled into the parking lot of the hospital, Dan and I got out and headed toward the visitor's entrance. He went through the revolving door first. I pulled the strings of my hood a little tighter and followed. When we got inside, we saw that there wasn't a secretary or volunteer sitting at the visitor's desk. There was a cop.

"Can I help you?" he said.

"We're here to see Ellen Howe. She was in the ICU yesterday."

The cop looked down the patient list. When he found the name, he straightened up in his chair. The vein at his temple seemed to twitch. He looked up at Dan and then over to me. It was like he was trying to look through the sunglasses into my eyes.

"I'll need some ID," he said.

"Okay." Dan produced his wallet and gave

the cop his driver's license out of it. I handed over my school ID which I usually try not to show to anybody. It has this horrible picture where I look like I have horse teeth. I didn't have much choice this time.

He took a quick glance at Dan's, but he held mine up as he looked at me.

"Would you mind removing your hood and glasses?"

"What for?"

The cop was still focused on my face. "There's a security issue with the patient you want to see. As you should know, Detective Marisconi has us on the lookout for your brother."

"You don't think he'd be crazy enough to come here, do you?"

The cop whistled. "Crazy?"

"Just do what he says, Nathan," Dan said.

I removed my hood, the Nats cap, and my sunglasses. I stood there while the cop held up my ID and glanced at it, then back at me. Then he took a piece of paper out of the drawer and held it up on the other side. I had no doubt it was a copy of one of Brian's mug shots.

"Okay. Just doing my job." He put the paper back in the drawer. He took out a couple of visitor stickers and wrote our names on them. He wrote

Ma's room number, 416, on them.

"Please make sure these are visible at all times," he said.

Dan peeled the back and put the sticker on the front of his sport coat. I pressed mine onto the middle of my black sweatshirt.

As we got into the ICU, I pulled my hood up and put my sunglasses back on.

When we got in there, Ma was barely conscious. Her eyes were open, but they were unfocused. Her neck was extended and her head was back. She looked like she was in a lot of pain.

"Ma. It's me," I said. "It's me and Dan. We came to see you."

Ma groaned, but she couldn't move her head.

"Are you in a lot of pain?"

She made a groan that sounded like, "Uh-huh."

"I'm sorry, Ma. You just gotta be strong. You're gonna be better when they take care of this infection. You're gonna get stronger," I said.

She blinked. A single tear ran down Ma's cheek.

I lost it. I felt the air leave my lungs and my legs just gave. If Dan hadn't caught me, I'd have hit the floor like a dead body.

Dan held me up. He could feel the sobs coursing through my body, even though I tried to keep them silent. He tried to talk to cover the noises.

"Hi, Ellen. I'm sorry you're going through all of this. I really do hope you can fight this off," he said. I was able to breathe more deeply. I started to gain control of myself.

When I looked back up at Ma, she was trying to say something. It took her a few tries before I understood her. "Hand," she croaked.

I reached out and grabbed her hand. It was icy and limp. I squeezed her fingers, but she wasn't able to squeeze back.

"I'm sorry, Ma," I said. I didn't know what else to say. I could feel the tears on my cheeks again. I leaned in close to her ear. "I brought Brian here to see you."

Her eyes opened wide and she took a sharp breath.

"Don't worry. It's gonna be all right," I whispered gently into her ear.

I took a step back and sort of collapsed against Dan. I leaned up against his chest. "We gotta go," I whispered.

I started breathing hard. I could feel hot tears on my cheeks again, but instead of groaning or crying, I started coughing. I couldn't control it. I had to bend down and rest my elbows on my knees to try and catch my breath.

Dan pulled me upright. "Ellen, I better get

him out of here. Give us a few minutes. I'll try to get him to calm down and then we'll come back."

Dan held me up the whole way through the hospital. We moved very quickly through the lobby and past the visitor's desk. The cop was watching us intently as we passed.

"He's really had a shock," Dan said. "We'll be right back."

The cop nodded.

Normally, when you leave the hospital, you have to go back to the desk and give them your visitor pass. Dan and I still had ours.

We moved through the parking lot quickly. As I got into the passenger seat of Dan's Mercedes, I peeled off the sweatshirt and handed it to Brian. I gave him the hat and my sunglasses, too. He put them on and got out. He'd pulled the hat down and the hood up. The sunglasses were pressed tightly against his face. I couldn't see any of Brian's long hair inside the hood. When he straightened up, he looked like me, maybe just a little heavier. Hopefully he wasn't heavy enough for anyone to notice.

He slouched a little and leaned against Dan as they walked back toward the hospital. This was it. All there was to do now was wait.

I sat with my body twisted in the seat so I

could see the hospital entrance behind us. I watched for several minutes for any sign of commotion or anything. I was rubbing my cheeks dry just to give my hand something to do. I'd never been more nervous in my whole life.

Nothing was happening. Maybe he'd really gotten in.

I waited. Time seemed to have stopped. I fought the urge to look at my phone for a long time. I finally gave in.

I looked down at my phone. They'd been gone for eight minutes. It wouldn't be long now. We agreed that Brian couldn't stay any more than ten minutes or else someone might recognize him. But if he got past the cop at the security desk, we were pretty much home free.

I almost jumped out of my skin when I heard the knock on the window.

I turned and saw the fleshy, pockmarked face of Frank Marisconi staring at me through the glass.

Oh, shit.

I fumbled at the door handle and opened it. I got out and faced him.

"How is she, Nathan?" he said.

I didn't answer right away. I looked him up and down. His face was droopy and tired. There was a small spot of lather on the corner of his lip. His shoulders sagged. It looked like a stiff wind would blow him over.

He wasn't on alert. He looked old and sad—maybe even drunk.

I took a couple of steps away from him. I circled around so that he would have to turn his back on the hospital entrance in order to follow me. He did. When I looked up, I saw them appear right behind Marisconi's head out of the revolving door—first Brian, then Dan.

They were headed right for us.

I yelled as loud and as fiercely as I could. "What the fuck do you care, Marisconi?" I didn't take my eyes from Marisconi's face. I didn't want him to turn around. I saw Brian make a quick move to one side and he was out of my line of vision. I couldn't let my eyes follow him. I just had to hope he was gone. Dan continued walking toward me. He was twirling his car keys around his finger.

Dan didn't say anything until he was right behind Marisconi. "Are you hassling him again, Frank?"

"Relax, you two. I was just asking how Ellen was," he said. Marisconi put his hand up to shield his eyes from the setting sun as he looked at Dan.

"She's not doing real good. Things are touch

and go. We appreciate the concern, though," Dan said.

"What are you doing here anyway? Didn't you ditch Ellen years ago? Suddenly you're bailing her kid out of jail and visiting her in the hospital." Marisconi was trying to be a hard-ass, but his heart just wasn't in it today.

"Just helping a sick friend," Dan said. He unlocked the car. "C'mon, Nate. Let's go."

We got into the car and when I looked in the side mirror, Marisconi had stalked off toward the hospital entrance.

"Is he still there?" Dan asked.

I had to duck low and to the side to keep Marisconi in the mirror. "He's heading toward the hospital."

"Can you see Brian?" Dan said.

"No."

"He ran off toward the aisle on the right when we heard you screaming at Marisconi. Let's wait until Marisconi is inside and then we'll find him," Dan said.

We did. Dan drove slowly through the lot and we looked between cars. Right near the entrance we saw Brian, squatting down against the wheel of a pickup truck. He had his head down. Dan stopped the car. I opened the door and slid into the backseat.

147

Brian didn't move.

"Bri!" I whispered loudly. His head shot up and he ran to us. He jumped in the car, slammed the door, and slumped down in the seat. Dan turned out of the lot and headed toward the beach across town. Nobody said anything, but we all knew there was nowhere for Brian to go except back to the cave.

Once Dan wheeled the Mercedes onto Old Mill Road, Brian sat up and turned back toward me. I had been looking at Grayson's Garage when I noticed he was looking at me.

"I'm going to turn myself in," he said.

"What?"

"I'm gonna turn myself in. I said good-bye to Ma in there. She couldn't move, but I know she understood. Tears came down her face and she groaned a little." Brian's voice cracked just the tiniest bit when he said the word "groaned," but he wasn't crying anymore.

I'd seen Brian focused before, but usually in preparation to hurt someone. His anger usually gave him focus. Something else was giving him focus this time.

"Are you sure?" I could hear the wavering in my own voice.

"Yeah. It's the only way, Nate," he said.

Dan spoke up. "Brian, you do realize you're

an adult? You'll be charged with murder. You could get the chair."

"Yeah. I know." Brian put his head down. "It doesn't matter. I've got to go away. I'm dangerous to everyone. All I've ever done is hurt the people I love. Whatever I get, I deserve it."

I could feel the words rising in my throat. I wanted to argue. I wanted to tell Brian that he was wrong, that he was a good person—that I loved him. But I didn't.

I sat there silently, staring at him.

He finally looked up at me. We stared at each other for a while. His eyes were the same glassy blue as Ma's, except his were young and alert. And they were gentle. When Brian was himself, when he wasn't charged by his anger like it was electricity, his eyes were calm and kind. I never asked Shannon about it, but she must have seen hope for Brian in those bright and gentle eyes.

If only...

"Do you...do you want to go now?" I said.

"No. Tomorrow. I just want one more night as a free man. I want to sit on the beach under the stars. It'll be a long time before I can do that again," he said.

"I'll go with you," I said. "I'll stay with you in the cave tonight. And then I'll go with you to the police station in the morning."

Brian shook his head. "I just wanna be alone tonight, little bro."

I was about to argue, but I didn't. If Brian wanted to be alone tonight, I could at least give him that.

"Well, at least let me pick you up in the morning and go with you to the police station?" I pleaded. For that moment, it was like we were little kids again. I was pleading with Brian to let me tag along.

"Okay, Nate." In the end, Brian always let me come with him.

"I can come, too," Dan said. "I'm supposed to leave for Clearwater tomorrow, but I can drive you boys to the station first. I can make sure Marisconi stays in line." Dan put the car in park. We were in front of the parking lot at the beach.

"No, that's okay, Dan. You've done enough already." Brian paused and looked down. Then he looked back up at Dan. "You've been a really big help through all this. I just want you to know…"

Brian wasn't used to this sort of thing. He didn't know how to thank people.

"We really appreciate your help, Dan," I said.

"Yeah. And I just wanna say I'm sorry for…"

Brian stopped. His forehead wrinkled. How could Brian possibly put into words what he was sorry for? "I'm just sorry, Dan."

Dan smiled. "Me too."

Brian opened the car door.

"Hold on." I pushed Brian's seat forward and got out. I looked around. There was no one there. "We're not even being careful," I said.

"Who cares if they catch me now anyway?" Brian said. He got out and looked up at the sky. It was getting dark. I glanced at my phone to see what time it was, but the phone was dead.

I turned to the front seat. I reached under it and brought out a plastic bag with three cans of food in it. I'd taken the last cans we had out of the pantry earlier that morning.

"Here. There's just a few in there, but you won't need much more," I said.

"Yeah. Guess not." Brian took the bag.

I turned to get in the front seat. "I'll be here in the morning. I'll try to get here at sunrise," I said over my shoulder.

Suddenly, Brian grabbed my shoulder. I stopped and turned to face my older brother.

"Thank you, Nate. Thanks for taking care of me," he said.

Then I hugged him. I don't know why I did

151

it, but I'm glad I did. He hugged me back. When we separated, he messed my hair with his big hand. "Sunrise, little bro," he said. He gave me his signature grin.

"Sunrise."

Chapter Eleven

When Dan pulled up in front of our house, he tried to assure me that Brian turning himself was the best possible thing.

"What else is he gonna do? Live in that cave forever?" Dan asked.

I wished he could. Brian could stay in the cave and then he couldn't hurt anyone. And no one could find him and hurt him either. But that was the kid in me talking. The fifteen-year-old knew different.

The house was pitch black when I came in. When I turned on the lights, it was a mess. I forgot that the last people here were the paramedics who took Ma to the hospital. The end table with the phone on it was knocked over. That was probably Ma, though. She probably collapsed right there.

There were boot prints from one of the

153

paramedics on the kitchen floor and I could hear the television in Ma's room was still on. I went and turned it off. I sat on Ma's bed. It smelled like Winstons, sweat, and piss.

It took me about an hour to clean up everything in the house. I changed the sheets on all the beds. I dusted, mopped, vacuumed. I took out the garbage. I figured Ma would like it tidy when she came home — if she came home.

Once I was done, I took a shower. It felt good to be clean. I went over to the couch and picked up my phone. Of course, it was still dead. I found the charger in my desk drawer and plugged it in.

There was only one message. It was a voice mail. I clicked the button to play it.

"So, Nathan. I waited by the trophy case for like twenty minutes yesterday, but I couldn't wait any longer. I had to be home when my sister got there." It was Celia's voice. It wasn't angry. It was awkward. "I was kind of looking forward to walking home with you," she said. I could hear the disappointment in her voice.

"I hope everything is okay. I know things are crazy for you right now. Call me when you get this message." She paused and took a breath. "You know…if you want to."

I hit the callback button.

What was I going to say? How was I going to explain any of this?

"Hello?" Celia's voice sounded tense.

"Hi, Celia. It's Nathan. Listen, I'm sorry I didn't meet you at the trophy case yesterday. Something happened and I had to leave school early."

"Are you okay? You didn't come to the library today either." I didn't want to worry her, but there was a part of me that really liked to hear her sounding worried about me.

"Yeah. I guess I'm okay, but I couldn't come to school today." I took a deep breath. "I know it's kinda late, but I was wondering if I could come over and see you?"

"Now?" she said. But I thought I could hear just the slightest hint of excitement. "Well…okay, I guess."

She gave me her address. She lived just about three blocks from us.

"I promise I'll be there in ten minutes. I'll never stand you up again," I said.

She laughed. "You better not."

I was wearing shorts, but I knew it was chilly enough that I'd need a sweatshirt. I looked around for my black hoodie. It wasn't in the hamper or in my closet. Then I remembered that Brian had it.

155

Well, I supposed that he needed it more than I did, especially on a night like tonight. I found a thick, gray flannel shirt in Brian's closet. I buttoned it up and headed out into the night.

As I came up Celia's street, I saw there was one white frame house in the middle of the block with its porch light on. As I came closer, I saw someone sitting on the stairs, huddled against the chill. I knew it was Celia. Once I passed under the streetlight closer to her house, she waved at me.

I came up and sat next to her on the stairs.

"I hope you don't mind sitting out here," she said. "My parents are asleep. I don't think they'd like to wake up and find I brought a guy into the house."

I laughed. "No."

I looked at Celia. She was wearing sweatpants and a University of Virginia sweatshirt that was about two sizes too big for her. She had on a knit cap with a panda face on the front of it. It looked like I had caught her right before she was going to bed herself.

"Are you planning to go to UVA?" I pointed at the sweatshirt.

"Yeah, right," she said. "Maybe if my parents win the lottery." A strand of her dark hair fell into her face. She tucked it behind her ear.

That was all I had. We sat in silence for a few moments until Celia finally asked, "What happened yesterday?"

"Well, that new dean was waiting for me when I got to sixth period. The hospital called school. They had to rush my mother there in an ambulance."

"Oh, my God. Is she all right?"

"Not really. She's in a lot of pain. They don't know if she has an infection or something. She could barely talk when I went to see her." I could feel my eyes burning.

"Is she gonna be all right?" Celia, genuinely concerned, put her hand on my knee.

"I don't know. It depends if they can find out what's wrong with her. Her immune system is so weak from chemo that any sort of infection is a huge deal. A bad cold could kill her." I felt tears on my cheeks, but I didn't want to lose it. I didn't want to start sobbing. I wanted to talk. I wanted to tell Celia all about it.

So I did. I told her everything. I told her about Brian getting in trouble all the time. I told her about Ma and Dan Howe. I told her about Shannon. And even though I wasn't sure I should, I told her everything—even about being in love with Shannon. I paused after that and looked at Celia. I expected her to look confused or angry, but she just looked sad.

"And that was the girl who died? The one your brother killed?"

I nodded.

"Oh, Nathan, I'm sorry."

Then I told her about the night of the party. I told her about Joe Runnel and the fight. I told her about hearing Brian and Shannon doing it in the basement. I even told her about kissing Shannon.

I stopped for a while after that. I needed to catch my breath.

Suddenly, I felt Celia's warm hand on the back of my neck. She pulled me close to her. "I'm so sorry about all of this, Nate." She smelled like apple-cinnamon shampoo. I laid my head on her shoulder and put my arms around her. She was warm.

She whispered in my ear. "You don't have to tell me any more if you don't want to."

But I did.   I told her about the next morning and seeing Joe Runnel run from out front of Shannon's house when Brian pulled up.

And I told her about Brian losing it and me falling over the coffee table and watching my brother rip the hammer from Shannon's hand and hit her with it.

I looked up at Celia when I described the sound. "It was like the sound of an egg cracking," I said. She winced.

I told her everything after that, too. I told her where the truck was hidden. I told her about being arrested and Dan coming to get me out. I told her about sneaking Brian into the hospital and how he was going to turn himself in.

Hell, I even told her about cleaning the house when I got home tonight.

When I was done, we just sat there for a while in silence. I could hear Celia's breathing. She stroked my hair gently.

After a long while, I looked up at her. Her face was calm. She was still stroking my hair. "I remember that after my sister died, my grandmother held me and stroked my hair like this. It didn't make me feel better. I was still sick that my sister was gone, but it just reminded me that someone cared."

"No, it's okay. It's good."

I glanced at my phone. It was nearly two a.m. "Listen, Celia, I'm sorry, but I better — "

"It's okay," Celia said. "I should get some sleep, too. Just promise that you'll call me later and let me know what happened. I want to make sure you're okay."

I felt the corners of my mouth turn up in a smile.

"What is that?" Celia asked. She had a sort of amused, confused look on her face.

"It's just that...I don't know. It's just funny. You're so worried about me and we only met two days ago."

"Yeah, I guess it is kinda funny." Suddenly, she tried to put a serious look on her face. "You know, you haven't even asked me out yet."

"Celia, would you—"

Before I could finish, Celia leaned over and kissed me. We kissed for a long time. I wasn't really sure what I was doing. I remember when I was about twelve years old, I asked Brian how to kiss a girl.

He'd said, "Just don't get too excited. Go slow and don't move around too much." I tried to follow that advice as best I could.

When we finished, Celia didn't burst out laughing, so I took that as a good sign.

As I walked home in the early morning, all I could think of was how I was going to tell Brian all about how his advice seemed to work. I mean, I remember the old saying that a gentleman doesn't kiss and tell, but I figured Brian would want to know that I had something good going for me.

I wanted him to know that I was going to be all right.

CHAPTER TWELVE

When I got home, I tried to go right to sleep, but I couldn't. I couldn't stop thinking about Celia. I lay in bed thinking about her. Her warm hand on the back of my neck, the scent of her hair. I kept replaying our kiss over and over. At one point, I got so lost in the memory that I found myself twirling my tongue gently around the inside of my mouth.

When I realized I was doing that, I actually laughed. I wanted to get up in the morning and see her again, but I knew I couldn't.

This was the day. Brian was going to turn himself in and after that was settled, I was going to the hospital to see Ma. The lives of the two most important people in my life were at stake. My stomach lurched as I thought about what would happen when Marisconi got ahold of Brian. Would he bring Shannon's parents down to the station to face him, too? I didn't know what was going to happen today, but I tried to keep the memory of Celia's soft hair and warm lips in my mind. It was the only thing that would keep me from going crazy.

I rolled around in bed. I don't think I slept at all. I got up in the dark and dressed slowly. The crisp moonlight through my bedroom window gave enough light for me to find my clothes. I went out into the kitchen and had some cereal. I figured I had better eat. It was going to be a long day.

I never turned the lights on at all. I wanted it to stay dark. I didn't want sunrise to come.

By the time I got ready, it was just after four a.m. I checked my phone. It was fully charged. Celia and Dan had asked me to call them after I finished at the police station. They wanted to know what happened with Brian. I stuck the phone in my pocket.

I went to the front door. I paused in the calm, safe dark for a moment before I set off into the cold morning.

I put Brian's gray flannel back on and headed out the door. I walked slowly toward the beach. The early morning walk toward the water looked exactly like I remembered it from when Brian and I were kids.

No excitement this time, though. No building castles in the sand. Brian would be lucky to get life in prison. This was a cold walk toward the end.

As I came up on the parking lot by the beach, I looked around. There was one car parked across the street from the lot—an old Ford. I walked up and looked inside the window. There was no one hiding in it. I scanned the rest of the street. I couldn't see anyone. I was alone.

I cut across the parking lot and up onto the path. I went slowly. The bumpy sand could be dangerous in the dark. When I reached the entrance to the cave, I stopped. I didn't even have to look down to find the opening. I knew it by heart.

I dropped onto my hands and knees and crawled in. It was as black as pitch. After a few crawling strides into the dark, I stopped and listened. I couldn't hear Brian breathing or snoring.

I crawled into the center of the cave and felt around the clammy floor for the light. My palm slid across its cold plastic top and I pressed down. The cave lit up. It took a few moments for my eyes to adjust. I scanned slowly along the walls of the cave and there was nothing. Brian wasn't there.

I looked back down and right next to the light were the two thin blankets I had brought Brian. They were neatly folded into rectangles and piled one on top of the other. On the top of the blankets was the rusty, worn bayonet that Brian and I had fought over on this beach so many years ago. I looked farther down and I saw something scrawled in the sand.

It looked like when a kid gets a tree branch and uses it to write his name in the sand. Except what I saw was my own name. Right below the blankets and the bayonet were just two words: *For Nate.*

I reached out and picked up the bayonet. I held it for a moment and then tossed it aside. I picked up both blankets and unfolded them, looking for any sign of Brian. Was there a note? Did he run away? Why wouldn't he have told me? I would've tried to help him get out of town. Had he already left and gone to the police station?

I scrambled back through the opening to the cave and I was about to run back toward the parking lot when I thought maybe Brian was simply sitting in the sand and looking up at the sky. That's what he said he was going to do. So instead of turning left, I turned right and headed toward the water. Once I was off the muddy sand of the path and I was up on the beach, the sliver of early morning sun revealed one set of footprints.

Tourist season was over and it was cold enough that even local kids weren't coming to the beach anymore. I knew the prints were Brian's. I followed them straight toward the water. The prints ended where the tide soaked the sand.

Sitting neatly right at the edge of the tide line were the white gym shoes Brian had worn yesterday. His socks were stuffed in them. I picked one of them up and looked at it closely, as if some detail on the shoe might reveal everything I needed to know.

That's when I understood.

I imagined Brian sitting on the sand, taking off his shoes and socks, and then carefully rolling up his pant legs. I imagined him staring out at the dark water as he slowly started to wade out into the Chesapeake. I imagined that same grim, determined look he had on his face yesterday in the car as he walked toward his death.

I imagine he kept walking until the water was too deep and then he started swimming out into the darkness. If there's one thing I know about Brian, he never looks back.

I sat there on the sand as the sun came up. I kept my gaze on the sea. I told myself that it was because I was looking for a sign of my brother swimming, laboring hard to get back to the shore. But I knew it wasn't. I knew I was gazing out at the water and letting the cold sunrise color my face because there was nothing else to do.

Brian was gone.

I was alone.

I sat there in the sand for an hour or so. I picked up Brian's shoes and carried them back to the cave. I crawled into the cave and picked up his blankets. I folded them again. I piled them neatly and put his shoes on top of the pile. Then I reached over and rubbed away the words Brian had scrawled into the sand. There was something satisfying about watching my own name disappear.

I put the blankets and shoes under my arm and did my best to crawl back to the opening. I had just reached it when I realized that I'd left the light on. When I looked back toward the light, the glint of metal caught my eye from the corner of the cave — the bayonet. I retrieved it, turned off the light, and brought everything out of the cave. I headed back up the path one more time toward the water.

Once more I followed Brian's footsteps to where he'd removed his shoes and socks. I placed the blankets and Brian's shoes gently on the sand. Then I took out the bayonet. I looked at it for a moment. I looked at the scratches and the patches of rust along the blade. I pressed the blade against my forehead. It was cold.

Then, I reeled back and threw it with all my

might out into the bay. It didn't go that far, really. I watched it tumble through the air, end over end for a second or two, and then cut into the water. Just like Brian, it was gone.

I looked down at Brian's shoes.

I thought about it. What it would feel like to walk out there myself? To walk until the dark water swallowed me?

Then I thought about Ma. I knew she needed me. I knew I had to get to the hospital.

And I thought about Celia. I'd promised never to stand her up again.

I sighed, picked up the blankets and shoes, and headed back toward the trail.

All the way home I thought about one of the last conversations I had with Brian in the cave. When I told him about being in love with Shannon and we had the fight where I almost killed him with the bayonet.

I remember I called him the hydra because the problems around him always seemed to multiply, just like the heads of that monster. As I walked through the empty streets of Wilton that morning, I thought that maybe Brian wasn't really like the hydra at all. He didn't seek out people to destroy. He didn't try to ruin people's lives for his own satisfaction.

Instead, maybe Brian was more like Hercules himself. The guy who would lose control of himself sometimes, and hurt those people he loved the most—like when Hercules killed his family and had to do the twelve labors to make up for it.

Just like Hercules, Brian could feel. In fact, he may have felt more than most people. His love, anger, loyalty, and guilt were all overwhelming.

And just like Hercules, Brian spent his whole life trying to make up for his mistakes. But he couldn't. He wasn't a hero with the power of the gods running through his veins.

He was just my brother.

The rest of that day is a blur. I brought Brian's stuff back home and placed it on his freshly made bed.

I'd promised both Celia and Dan I'd call them after I'd taken Brian to the police station. Celia didn't expect me to call her until later. She was at school anyway, but Dan wanted me to call right away. He said he wasn't going to leave for Clearwater until the afternoon just because he wanted to make sure everything was okay with Brian and Ma before he left.

How could I tell them?

So I sent Dan and Celia a text—the same text, actually—*"Brian's gone."*

Celia responded right away. "I'm sorry," was all her message said.

About thirty seconds after that, the phone rang. It was Dan. I let it go to voice mail. He called again and I let it go again. The third time he called I turned off my phone. I wasn't ready to talk.

I walked down to the bus stop and took the bus to Duffle County Hospital.

When I walked into the lobby, a different police officer sat at the desk. I handed him my ID and let him eyeball me. He shrugged and gave me back my ID. He wrote out my visitor's pass. I moved through the hospital slowly. I wanted to see my mother and make sure she was okay. But would she ask me about Brian? And if she did, what would I say?

When I reached the ICU, a nurse was with Ma. The nurse whispered her report to me while Ma slept. She told me they discovered some water in her lungs and drained it. They were also keeping up antibiotics in her IV. The infection seemed to be under control. Her temperature was almost normal. She was a little better today. Ma had said a few words and taken a few spoonfuls of soup. She was still tired, though. I sat in the chair across from Ma while the nurse left to check other patients.

Ma's eyes opened. They were the same glassy blue as Brian's.

I stood up and leaned close to her so she could see me.

"Hi, Ma."

"Nathan?"

"Yeah, Ma. It's me. How are you today? You look better than yesterday."

She sort of shrugged as best she could. Her eyes looked directly into mine. She reached up her hand. I took it. It was still icy cold.

"Brian?" she said.

I looked down.

"Brian?" she said again.

I shook my head. "No, Ma. He's gone."

"For good?"

I nodded. I still couldn't look at her.

I heard one soft sob and then Ma's hand squeezed mine.

"Just us," Ma said. It wasn't a question.

I looked up at her. There were tears on her cheeks, but she wasn't losing it. There was something in her eyes — strength.

I wiped my eyes with the back of my hand. "Yeah, Ma. Just us."

We didn't say anything after that. We just stared at each other for a long while. I kept holding my mother's hand. I smelled the rubbing alcohol. I heard the beeping of machines. I felt the steady

171

pressure of my mother's hand in mine.
   I think Ma had decided what she was living for.

Epilogue

I walked slowly to the bus stop that afternoon. The rain came down slow and steady as I crossed Melton Avenue. The summer was long gone. I took a lunging step over a puddle at the curb so I could get into the bus shelter. When the bus finally pulled up, I got on and sat against the window in the back.

I took out my phone and flipped through the texts. The last one was from Dan.

The text read, "How was work today?"

"Not bad. Getting close to closing up for winter," I responded.

"Good. Then you can focus on school," he sent back.

Dan had gotten me a job at the Champagne, one of the big resorts. It was sort of far from home on the north end of town, but after everything that happened, no one was willing to give me another job.

I guess being the little brother of a murderer didn't make me a very attractive candidate.

Dan got me in on the grounds crew at the resort. Right now we're doing all sorts of maintenance to get the grounds ready for winter. It's sort of a short-term job because they'll lay me off in the winter, but it's good money. I spend most of my Saturdays and Sundays digging up bushes, laying sod, and raking leaves.

It's actually good work for me. I don't have to talk to people very much. I have time to think.

And Dan's been really cool since all this happened. He got me the job and he promised to help me pay for college if I can get in. My grades were for shit through the beginning of the school year while I was going through everything with Brian. But I've been working hard to get them straightened out these past couple of months.

Dan hunts me down whenever he comes to the resort and I'm working. He usually takes me for lunch at the restaurant in the Champagne. The restaurant's kind of fancy and I always feel out of place in my dirty work clothes. Dan always tells me not to worry about how I look. While we eat, he asks me about what I'm learning and whether or not I'm caught up at school.

He's even stopped by the house and had dinner with me and Ma a couple of times. Don't get me wrong, he and Ma are never going to get back together or anything like that, but Dan's sort of a part of our family again. I don't think any of us realized how much we missed each other.

When the bus finally squealed to a halt in front of the beach, I got out and began the short walk home. The whole way I thought about Brian. Actually, that's not right. The whole way home I thought about the day after Brian died.

I slept at the hospital the night Brian died. The nurse brought in an armchair and I pulled it close to Ma's bed so I could hold her hand. The chair was uncomfortable, so I didn't sleep much, but I was asleep when Marisconi came in the next morning.

I woke up when Marisconi shook my shoulder. "Nathan, wake up," he said. His voice wasn't angry that morning. When I opened my eyes and looked into his face, I knew why he'd come.

Ma was already awake and staring at him.

"Listen, Ellen, Brian's body washed up on the shore this morning. He drowned in the bay. We're not sure yet, but we think it was suicide," he said quickly, but gently. After all this, even Marisconi was trying to show us some pity. He also told us

175

that they'd found Brian's truck, too. Marisconi said that it would be impounded for a few weeks, but that he'd make sure we got it back.

Ma and I both already knew that Brian was gone, but we cried anyway after Marisconi told us. It was like hearing the words made it real. I didn't ask Ma how she felt. I know that when I finally stopped crying, I felt empty. Like I would never feel anything again—happiness, pain, fear—nothing. I actually felt like that for a while.

Ma's health got better and after about a week they let her go home. I stayed home with her for a few days to make sure she could manage, but she quickly built up enough strength to move around on her own. She made me go back to school.

The first day back was like that Monday after Brian had killed Shannon. I could feel everyone looking at me, but this time it was different. I think people felt bad for me this time. There were no whispers behind my back or accusing questions. In fact, no one said anything to me. No one except Celia. She stuck with me as much as she could during the day and walked me to all of my classes. Every time I felt an uncomfortable stare, Celia would squeeze my hand just to let me know she was there.

Actually, there was one other person who talked to me that day—the school social worker. I got called out of second period and Ms. Hathaway brought me into her office. She's a chubby, older woman with curly brown hair. As she sat behind her desk, she gave me a little speech about how I'd been through a lot. She used the word "traumatic" eleven times. I actually counted.

At first, I didn't want to talk to her at all, but she kept at it. She called me out of second period every day that week. I sat in her office for a couple of days without saying a word.

I told Ma about it and she said something that changed my mind about Ms. Hathaway. She said, "You know, those counselors and social workers were always trying to get to Brian. I thought I was protecting him by keeping them away from him. Maybe things woulda been different if he'd have talked to someone."

So I went in the next morning and I started talking to Ms. Hathaway. At first, we just talked about what happened with Brian. Then one day, I told her how I felt guilty because even though he was a murderer, I just wanted my brother back.

I'll never forget what Ms. Hathaway said. "It's okay for you to miss him, Nathan. It doesn't make you a bad person because you loved your brother unconditionally."

Now I actually tell her a lot of the good stuff

177

about growing up with Brian and it makes me feel better. I've got a regular appointment with her on Wednesdays after school.

There's one thing that's still eating at me about the morning of the murder, though—Joe Runnel. I still don't know why he didn't tell Marisconi that I was in the truck with Brian. Did he really run away so fast that he didn't notice me? I've talked about this with Celia a lot. She keeps telling me that I can't worry about it anymore. It's over. But every time I see Joe Runnel in the hallway, I wonder. Could he tell on me now? What would happen if he did? I hope I never find out.

I finally stood in front of the door to our house. I could hear laughter from inside. I smiled. It had been a long time since we had laughter in our house.

I opened the door and Ma and Celia were sitting at the table. Celia was telling her about her uncle in Mexico who once owned a pet monkey. Her uncle came home one day to find the monkey had pooped everywhere. It was a funny story. Celia told it well, too. She built it up by describing all of these places her uncle discovered poop, and one was more hilarious than the next. I stood in the doorway and didn't say anything. I'd heard the story a couple of times already, but I loved seeing

Celia get all worked up and making these disgusted faces every time she described somewhere the monkey had gone.

And it was good to hear Ma laugh. Her laugh was still thin, sort of wheezy, but it was real.

Celia's little sister, Natalia, was sitting on the couch, texting. She looked up at me when I came in. I put my finger up to my lips to show her that I didn't want to interrupt Celia. She shook her head, but gave a little smile. She was Celia in miniature, except with curly hair. She was a good kid, really smart, too. Celia brought her over a lot when she came to our place. Celia told me that her mom always tells her to take Natalia with her when she comes over. I don't mind. I really don't.

A couple of weeks ago, Celia told me she finally figured out why her mother always wants her to bring Natalia with her to my house.

We had been standing in front of my locker before school. "I think it's a form of birth control. I think she figures I won't sleep with you if my sister's around," she said. I laughed about that one for a while.

Finally, Celia finished telling my mother the monkey story and looked up at me. "Hi, Nate," she said.

Ma turned in the chair. "Hi, sweetheart. We

179

waited for you to eat. Are you hungry?" Ma got up and went into the kitchen.

Celia walked toward me. She looked over her shoulder and saw that my mother's back was turned. She reached up and kissed me. Natalia made a vomiting noise from the couch.

"You shut up," Celia said, pointing at her sister, but the corners of Celia's mouth betrayed a smile.

Celia turned back to me. "How are you?"

I'm still never sure how to answer that question when someone asks me. There are times I still feel terribly guilty. There are times that I think I don't deserve anything at all—Dan's friendship, Ma's improving health, Celia's attention. Hell, there are times I think I don't deserve to be alive.

And sometimes, I just really miss my brother.

But I know that I've got to keep going or else I'll get swallowed up, too.

I looked down into Celia's soft brown eyes. "I think I'm all right," I said.

I was really trying to be. Maybe, just maybe, I was going to be.

About the Author

This is the debut novel from Patrick Iovinelli. He teaches courses in language, literature, and science fiction at a large public high school. He is also a musician, baseball fanatic, and little brother. He lives in the Chicago suburbs with his wife, two daughters, and a beagle.